CORNERED!

Jim Waggoner broke into a run. A large-caliber gun popped behind him and then another shot was fired, but the men were shooting in the dark so he kept running.

"God damn it, git after 'im."

"I'm runnin' as fast as I can!"

Bending low, Jim ran into the tall grasses and weeds that grew along Apache Creek. A moment later he stumbled into a downed tree, barking his knees painfully, and fell across it. He lay there for a moment, trying to get his wind. Even though the night was black he knew it was just a matter of time before they found him. Thinking of that made him grip the butt of the Army Colt a little tighter.

"I recollect an old blowed-down cottonwood over there. I bet he's behind it!"

They were moving. They were coming. Jim Waggoner believed he was going to die. All he could do now was kill as many of those sons of bitches as he could before they got him. He hadn't come back to Apache Creek to kill anyone, but it looked like he had no choice. He was ready to kill.

FOR THE BEST OF THE WEST—
DAN PARKINSON

A MAN CALLED WOLF   (2794, $3.95)
Somewhere in the scorched southwestern frontier where
civilization was just a step away from the dark ages, an
army of hired guns was restoring the blood cult of an an-
cient empire. Only one man could stop them: John
Thomas Wolf.

THE WAY TO WYOMING   (2411, $3.95)
Matt Hazlewood and Big Jim Tyson had fought side by
side wearing the gray ten years before. Now, with a bloody
range war closing in fast behind and killers up ahead,
they'd join up to ride and fight again in an untamed land
where there was just the plains, the dust, and the heat—
and the law of the gun!

GUNPOWDER WIND   (2456, $3.95)
by Dan Parkinson and David Hicks
War was brewing between the Anglo homesteaders and the
town's loco Mexican commander Colonel Piedras. Figur-
ing to keep the settlers occupied with a little Indian trouble, Piedras had Cherokee warrior Utsada gunned down in
cold blood. Now it was up to young Cooper Willoughby to
find him before the Cherokees hit the warpath!

THE WESTERING   (2559, $3.95)
There were laws against settin' a blood bounty on an innocent man, but Frank Kingston did it anyway, and Zack
Frost found himself hightailin' it out of Indiana with a
price on his head and a pack of bloodthirsty bounty
hunters hot on his trail!

DOYLE TRENT

APACHE CREEK AMBUSH

ZEBRA BOOKS
KENSINGTON PUBLISHING CORP.

ZEBRA BOOKS

are published by

Kensington Publishing Corp.
475 Park Avenue South
New York, NY 10016

First printing: February, 1991

Printed in the United States of America

Chapter One

The lump in his throat grew larger as he got closer to the place where it had happened. When he rode to the top of a low grassy hill and saw Apache Creek ahead, he reined up.

His pale eyes ignored the town a half mile to the west and the railroad running north of the creek. Instead, they studied the creek and the trees across a narrow wagon road five hundred yards ahead. Nothing alive was in sight. The prairie sun burned down and heat waves danced between him and the creek.

Was this the place? Was that the tree? He wanted to know. He didn't want to know.

For a long moment, he sat there, feeling his heart pound, his pulse race. He'd know the place if he saw it close-up. It lay in his mind like a germ that wouldn't die. For eleven years he'd been thinking about it. Now that he was here he had an urge to turn around and leave. To try to forget it.

With an unsteady hand he pushed his hat back and dragged a shirtsleeve across his sweat-dampened forehead. His breathing was shallow, his chest constricted. Resetting his hat, he reached a decision and urged the roan horse on. He couldn't go back. Not yet.

The horse carried its rider on a slow walk across the sandy road, over the short grass and prickly pear to the creek. It seemed to know that it was supposed to stop in the shade of a huge old cottonwood. The rider dismounted slowly, looked up at the horizontal limb twenty feet above the ground. This was the tree.

Removing his hat, he stood with his head bowed. The anger that had been a part of him for so long had finally subsided and he felt like bawling. His lips barely moved as he mumbled a short prayer, something he'd been taught by Mrs. Nance at the Double O Cowcamp.

Where were the graves? He dropped the reins, put his hat on, and walked among the tall sunflowers and hogweeds. Unless someone had put markers on them, the graves would be impossible to find. Eleven years of rain, snow, and growing weeds would have hidden them. Still, he walked in all directions, spurs dragging, looking. Nothing. They had to be buried here. There was no graveyard this side of Denver and no one would have transported the bodies that far. His chest tightened again. The bitterness was back.

His upper lip curled in anger as he thought, Two men were buried here and no one bothered to mark the graves.

Grim-faced, he gathered the reins, stepped into the saddle, and turned the roan horse east. He rode along the creek for a half mile before he stopped again. Not much was left of the one-room sod shack where the claims-court judge had lived with his wife. What was left was so badly charred it was unrecognizable. Tuttle was the judge's name. Chester Tuttle. The judge had kept land-claim records in a trunk in a corner of his room.

Riding on, he kept the creek between him and the remains. The closer he got to the Waggoner place the stronger was the urge to leave. He was gaining nothing by this. Just torturing himself. Yet, another force pulled him on until he reined up in front of what was left of a dugout. It was built into the side of a cutbank

6

that had been carved out by Apache Creek perhaps a thousand years ago. The dirt roof had caved in. The door was buried. Grass grew out of the roof.

Again he dismounted, a weary kind of sadness filling his chest. For a long moment he stood silent, remembering. Then as before he dropped the reins and walked, spurs ringing. He walked to the top of the cutbank above the dugout. There he found a grave, a familiar one. The wooden cross had been pushed over, probably by a grazing animal, and lay half-hidden in the grass. Hands trembling, he picked it up, brushed the dirt off and read the inscription carved on the horizontal piece:

MRS. MATILDA WAGGONER 1832 1860 WIFE MOTHER RIP

He couldn't keep a tear from running down his cheek as he stood there, hat off, head bowed. His lips barely moved as he mumbled another prayer.

Finally, he wiped his eyes with a shirtsleeve, put his hat on, and pushed the cross into the ground so it stood up straight. Then he walked back to his horse and mounted. Before he turned the horse west toward the town he'd seen in the distance, he took one more long look around, shaking his head sadly.

This had been his home.

Chapter Two

The blond young man riding a red roan horse down the main street of Apache Wells puzzled her. She had a feeling she should know him. Janet Carbaugh stood on the wide wooden porch of the Apache Wells Mercantile with a straw broom in her hands. Strangers were seldom seen here. The Kansas Pacific carried passengers to Denver, and stopped in Apache Wells only long enough to take on water from the high wooden tank west of town. Occasionally a new wagon or new rolls of galvanized wire ordered by a rancher were unloaded at the one-room depot, and occasionally a passenger climbed on board, headed for Denver. The only passengers who got off were those returning from Denver.

She watched the young man ride at a walk down the street, his eyes taking in everything. A rancher's freight wagon went by in the opposite direction followed by a one-horse buggy with a canvas top. For a second, her soft brown eyes met the young man's pale blue ones. Quickly, he looked away. She watched and studied him. No, she had never seen him before, and no, there was nothing familiar about him.

Yet there was something about him that pulled at the back of her mind. Something troubling.

He rode past the two blocks of business buildings with their wooden hitchrails in front. There were the

Prairie Rose saloon, Ma Baker's cafe, the harness and saddle shop, the laundry, the barber shop, the Apache County sheriff's office. At the sheriff's office he reined up and sat there a few seconds, as if trying to decide whether to dismount and go in. Then he went on.

The screen door behind her opened with squeaky springs, then slammed shut again as a man came out. "Evenin', Miss Carbaugh. Hot, ain't it." He was John Woods, who owned and operated the barber shop.

"Good evening, Mr. Woods. How is Mrs. Woods? I hear she isn't feeling so well."

"She's got the rheumitiz somethin' awful, but she gets around."

"I'm sorry to hear that. I hope she gets better."

"If she don't, I'm gonna send her over to Denver to a doctor over there." He walked down the two steps to the dusty street.

Finished with her sweeping, Janet Carbaugh started to go inside and paused when she saw the young man on the roan horse coming back. He was looking at her now and riding right toward her.

"Pardon me, ma'am," he said, stopping in front of the porch. "I wonder if you'd be so kind as to direct me to the nearest hotel." He had straw-colored hair thick around his ears under the black cattleman's hat, and blond eyebrows to go with the pale blue eyes.

"Why, I . . ." Why was she suddenly flustered? "I, uh, sir, there is no hotel here, but a Mrs. Jamison rents rooms to transients. Her house is one block north and two blocks west. It's the only two-story house in that block."

Why was she staring? Was he looking at her strangely too? Was it only because she was acting strange?

"Thank you," he said. "Is there a place where I can put up my horse?"

He was carrying a walnut-handled pistol in a holster on his right hip. But he appeared to be a well-mannered young man, not the rowdy troublemaking kind. "Why, yes, Mr. Butler has a barn and some pens near the creek, a block south and a block east. He takes care of horses for other folks."

"Thanks again, ma'am." He turned the roan horse away.

"It's Miss." She said it quickly without thinking, and immediately wished she hadn't. But it didn't matter. He was gone. The roan horse was traveling at a trot now.

It was early next morning when Janet Carbaugh saw the young man again. Her boss, Mr. Woodbine, had just opened the big iron safe and was putting money in the cash drawer to make change with. She was stocking a shelf with rolls of muslin. The front door opened and he came in.

"Good morning, young fella," Mr. Woodbine said cheerfully. "Out early, aren't you?"

"Yes sir," he said. He spoke pleasantly enough, but there was a tightness around his eyes and mouth. He'd just shaved, she could tell, and the straw-colored hair, what she could see of it under his hat, had recently been combed. "I need a shovel," he said. "A long-handled round point." He was a little above average in height, slender, with arms and shoulders well developed from hard labor.

"I'll get it," Janet said, hurrying to a back room. She wanted to wait on him herself, but she didn't understand why. Hurrying back, she handed him the shovel. "It's sixty-five cents."

"Gonna do some digging, are you?" Mr. Woodbine asked.

"Yes sir." He fished some coins out of his pants pocket, handed them to her, and started to leave.

Again she spoke without thinking, the words coming out in a rush: "You're new in town aren't you I'm Janet Carbaugh and this is Mr. Woodbine he owns this store." She couldn't let him leave without trying to learn his name.

But all he said was, "Pleased to meet you," and walked to the door, spurs ringing. Again he was gone.

"Not very talkative, is he?" Woodbine mused. She said nothing, only stared at the door he had just walked through. "And you, Janet, you look like you've seen a ghost. Or is it because there's a scarcity of young men around here?"

"Oh." She knew a combination of interest and bewilderment showed on her face. "It's nothing. It's really nothing at all."

Chapter Three

As he rode out of town, following the creek east, he looked back. Eleven years ago there'd been no town here and no railroad. He'd heard about the Kansas Pacific laying rail from somewhere in Kansas all the way to Denver, but he hadn't heard about the town. Apache Wells, it was called. Named after the creek, no doubt, which had been misnamed by some white man who saw Indians and mistook them for the Apaches he'd heard or read about. There were no Apaches around here. It was the Cheyennes and Arapahos who made life dangerous for white folks in this territory. But the name had stuck, and now a town carried the same name.

The town had probably gotten started by the Kansas Pacific as a place to house and feed railroad laborers. Somebody, maybe that Woodbine gent, had opened a general store, and the settlers had found that a convenient place to buy supplies. So a town had grown where eleven years ago the only thing that had broken the monotony of the low hills and shallow draws was the creek and a few trees growing along it. In fact, eleven years ago a grove of cottonwoods had stood near where the town now stood. Most of the trees had been chopped down, probably for firewood and building logs.

Progress. The young man had liked the trees. He'd liked climbing and playing in them. But before the railroad came it had been impossible to build a decent house here. There'd been too few trees to build log houses, and Denver was too far away to haul lumber from in wagons.

Now, with the railroad to do the hauling, folks who had the money could build fine houses, like that one over there on the other side of the Apache Creek bridge. It was a handsome wood-frame house, painted white, with a covered porch.

He rode on, carrying the shovel across the saddle in front of him. Colorado was now a territory and had an official state government and official county governments. It even had official courts, or so he'd heard.

Too bad there'd been no official courts eleven years ago. His jaw muscles bulged and his throat tightened when he thought about it.

A mile and a half from town, at the remains of the Waggoner dugout, he dismounted, loosened the cinches, and dropped the reins. The roan horse would graze, but it wouldn't wander far. Carrying the shovel, he climbed to the top of the cutbank and stood over the grave a moment, bareheaded, head bowed. Then he went back to the dugout, guessed where the door was buried, and started digging.

This was what he'd come here for, to visit the graves and see if he could find some kind of family memento, something that had belonged to the Waggoner family. He had in mind a wedding picture, a daguerreotype, of his mother and dad.

It was something he could touch.

It had taken him a long time to decide to come back. He'd wanted to forget the whole thing. Let it all stay buried. Go on with his life. Coming back would be painful. It could revive all the old anger and bitterness. He hadn't wanted that. But he couldn't get it out of his mind, and eventually, now that he was twenty-one, he had reached his decision.

The prairie soil was easy to dig in, and within an hour his shovel hit the top of the doorframe. He remembered

13

the doorframe being built of heavy logs dragged from the creek. Sweating, he took off his shirt and hat, and continued digging, standing on the shovel with both feet at times to push it farther into the dirt. The Army Colt was heavy and awkward on his hip, and he unbuckled the gunbelt and laid the gun and holster on top of his shirt. Soon he had enough of the door uncovered to look inside.

He was disappointed. Dirt from the caved-in roof had covered nearly everything.

On his knees, he peered in and saw the two-burner cast iron stove on its side with sections of stovepipe beside it. A piece of a wooden table and one chair were visible. Standing, he shoveled more dirt out of the door until he had a hole big enough to crawl through. He took a small tin box containing sulfur matches out of his shirt pocket and crawled into what used to be his home. The matches put out enough light that he could see one side of the bed where his mother and dad had slept, and one end of the bunk where he had slept with his uncle Tobe. But the far end of the room was completely covered with dirt. The wooden box that his mother had kept her wedding dress and a set of fine china in, was under a thousand pounds of prairie soil.

He remembered how his mother, on Sunday mornings, insisted that everyone drink coffee from those china cups, things she had inherited from her mother. He had to grin when he remembered—living like gophers in a dugout on the prairie and drinking coffee out of fine china cups. His mother intended to enjoy what little elegance she could.

Digging out that wooden box would take hours of hard labor, but he had to do it. Otherwise, his trip here would have been for nothing. He backed out of the hole and reached for the shovel. He stopped suddenly and stared, afraid to move.

He was staring into the bore of a big pistol held by a man with a square hard face.

Chapter Four

There were four of them, sitting their horses near the pile of dirt he had shoveled away from the dugout door. They were cattlemen, wearing high-top boots with their pant legs stuffed inside. Two of them had wide-brim hats with the brims rolled up on the sides. The other two wore flat-brim hats. And two of them had sixguns in their hands.

"Who are you and whatta you want?" said the oldest of the four. His square face sat on a thick neck, supported by wide shoulders. A thick gray mustache nearly covered a thin-lipped mouth.

The young man glanced down at his own sixgun on top of his shirt. It was a good two steps away.

"I ask you a question."

"Why, uh . . ." The gun barrels didn't waver.

"You're trespassin' and I got a right to shoot you where you stand."

"I'm, uh, I'm looking for something."

"What? What're you lookin' for?"

"Why, uh . . ." He didn't want to answer.

The oldest man took his eyes away long enough to study the red roan horse grazing nearby. The horse wore a brand that consisted of an overlapping double O. "Where'd you come from? Where'd you get that shovel? What're you lookin' for?"

Another man spoke, "I heard of that brand. That Double O. That's a Texas outfit. West Texas, I think."

"Answer me, boy, or we'll take you to town and let the

15

sheriff get it out of you."

"Yeah," said a third man. "Let 'im sweat it out in that hot box of a jail for a couple days and he'll do anything he's told to."

"Are you gonna answer me, boy?"

"I, uh . . ." He squared his shoulders and looked the older man in the eyes. "I don't think it's any of your business."

"He's got a smart mouth, Mr. Whitfield. Maybe we oughta give 'im a good whuppin' and send 'im on his way."

"That sheriff'd just fine 'im ever'thing he's got in his pockets and keep it hisself."

"Yeah, and if he ain't got nothin', he'd just run 'im out of town."

While they were talking, the young man's mind was working. Whitfield. Raymond Whitfield. Yeah. He was one of them. Early fifties now, gray around the ears. A little heavier. Ray Whitfield had been the loudest one of the bunch, the one who had complained the most. Yeah, this was Ray Whitfield.

The realization brought a bitter bile to the young man's throat. His chest constricted again and his heart beat faster. He could feel the old anger rising. It made his hands tremble. He put his hands on his hips to stop them from trembling.

"Say . . ." Whitfield was squinting at him, eyes nothing more than slits in his square face, "you wouldn't be . . . your name wouldn't be Waggoner, would it?"

"Yeah." The word came out in a bitter hiss. "My name is Waggoner. James B. Waggoner. Remember me, Mr. Whitfield?"

"Well, I'll be goddamned. I wondered if you was still alive. I wondered if you'd ever come back here."

"Now you know."

Whitfield looked at the other men. "You gents don't know this boy. We got shut of him a long time ago." Looking back at the young man, he said, "If you got any plans of gettin' even, you better forget it. We got laws here now and

16

a law officer that don't take no shit from no drifter. You best get on that horse over there and get long gone."

"If," one of the others said, "that is his horse. The Double O don't sell horses."

"Could of been stole."

"How'd you come by that horse, boy?"

"That's none of your damned business." His fists were clenched now. He wished the older man would get off his horse. He wanted to punch out at him, smash his face, stomp him flat. The anger was back. His whole body trembled with anger.

Then he reminded himself that he hadn't come here for revenge. He wanted no trouble. He had to control his anger, force it down. He tried to speak in a normal tone. It was difficult, but he managed. "Listen, I didn't steal that horse, I worked for him. I worked for the Double O for a long time, and I took that horse in place of two months' wages."

"You got a bill of sale?"

"Yeah. In my saddle pockets."

"Go get it."

"Why should I? If there's a county sheriff here, he's the one I'll show it to. How I got that horse is none of your damned business."

"All right. Put your shirt on. And don't touch that gun. Touch that gun and we'll blow holes in you."

"Whatta we gonna do with 'im, Ray?"

"Take 'im to town. Tell old Rogers to run 'im out of the country and make sure he stays out. He ain't nothin' but trouble."

"We could hang 'im for horse stealin'."

"Naw. We don't do that anymore. We got laws to do the hangin' now."

"Laws," one of the men grumbled. "I ain't seen no use for 'em yet." He dismounted from a bay horse and picked up James Waggoner's gunbelt. He hung the belt — gun, holster and all — over his saddle horn. Another man rode over to the roan, leaned down, picked up the bridle reins, and led the horse back.

"Get your shirt on."

Jim Waggoner slipped his shirt on, buttoned it, and shoved the tail into the waistband of his cotton pants. Another man pulled a lever-action rifle out of a saddle boot and held it pointed at him. It was a Henry repeating rifle, a Civil War Yankee gun that fired metallic cartridges.

"Get on your horse. And just try to run for it. I can put four shots in you before you get a hunnerd feet."

"It'd be a shame to accidental shoot that horse. He looks like a good 'un."

"I ain't gonna accidental shoot no horse. This gun shoots where I aim it."

It was embarrassing, riding down the main street of town, surrounded by four grim-faced men, his gunbelt hanging from someone else's saddle horn. Townspeople stared. The pretty, dark-haired, slender girl came out of the mercantile and stared. They halted in front of a one-story plank building with a sign hanging over the boardwalk in front of it. The sign read, APACHE COUNTY SHERIFF.

Whitfield dismounted and went inside. On foot, he was shorter than he looked horseback, and wider too. Yes, Jim Waggoner thought, he's the one. He's the one who started the whole thing. In less than a minute, Whitfield was back.

"Old Rogers ain't here. Left a note. He's gone to Denver. Won't be back till tomorrow."

"Well, what're we gonna do with 'im?"

Whitfield answered, "I got authority to arrest somebody when the sheriff ain't here. He appointed me a special deputy. I'm gonna lock him up."

"All right," the young man said with resignation, "if you're a duly appointed deputy sheriff I'll show you the bill of sale. It's right here in my saddlebags."

"You can show it to the sheriff when he gets back. Meantime, it'll do you good to spend a night in jail. Make you more'n happy to leave the country when you get out. And it'll keep you out of trouble."

"Whatta we gonna feed 'im?"

"Won't hurt him to miss a couple of meals. If he's got money, he can eat over at Ma Baker's place when the sheriff lets him out. And he can damn well pay for his horse's keep too. No sense in makin' the county pay."

"Haw. The damn county ain't got two nickels to rub together nohow."

Inside the sheriff's office was a rolltop desk, battered and scarred, two wanted posters on the wall, a gun rack holding a lever-action rifle and a double-barreled shotgun, locked with a big padlock, and two wooden chairs. James Waggoner was searched at gunpoint. A roll of bills was taken from a shirt pocket and a folding knife was taken from a hip pocket. That and a change of clothes and a few papers in his saddlebags were all he owned.

The man who took the money winked at another man. Then Jim Waggoner was shoved toward an iron door that connected the sheriff's office with a one-cell jail. By now, the young man was no longer able to hold down the anger. His voice quavered with it when he said, "Go choke yourselves, you sorry bunch of fools."

He was shoved through the door and the door was slammed shut. The walls were made of heavy timbers. A wooden bunk was against a wall, and a tin bucket stood under it. There was no window. A key turned with a loud click in the iron door. The men left.

He was alone.

He paced the floor. His jaws were clamped so tight his teeth hurt. With the iron door and the outside door closed, it was hot in the cell. The sun beat down on the roof, making an oven out of the building. Sweat ran down his face and made his armpits itch as he swore under his breath. Everything Mrs. Nance at the Double O Cowcamp had preached to him, everything old Zack Dawson had taught him, the promise he had made to himself, all were forgotten. He felt the same way he'd felt eleven years ago when he saw the bodies of his dad and uncle.

Chapter Five

Word spread quickly in the small town. Now she knew who he was. Though she'd never seen him before, she recognized the name. Waggoner. She'd heard the story about the double hanging and the boy who was left homeless. No one could remember the boy's first name. No one knew his first name. Her stepfather, Raymond Whitfield, refused to talk about it, but Mrs. Chester Tuttle had repeated the story to her twice, and Mrs. Jamison remembered the boy well.

Janet Carbaugh hadn't lived here then. Her widowed mother had met Raymond Whitfield at Fort Dodge years after the incident on Apache Creek. Mrs. Carbaugh's army officer husband had been killed in a skirmish with the Comanches, and she was destitute. When Whitfield, a cattle seller, proposed marriage and promised to make a good living for her and her child, she agreed and moved west to the Whitfield claim.

After the young girl had heard the story, she'd gone several times to the dugout where the Waggoners had lived. She'd tried to imagine what kind of people they were and what Mrs. Waggoner had looked like. The grave at the top of the cutbank fascinated her. Mrs. Waggoner had been killed by Indians, the same as her father. Each year since she was fourteen she had picked wild flowers and placed them on the grave. At first she'd refused to open the wooden box against the far wall of the dugout, feeling like an unwanted stranger intruding into someone else's lives. But eventually, when she was sixteen and saw the roof beginning to cave in, she opened the box and took the set of china cups and saucers to her room at the new ranch house.

There, she had packed it away carefully and hoped that one day a relative of the Waggoners would come to Apache Creek and would be happy to have a family heirloom.

Now the boy was grown and was back.

And he was in jail. He had stolen the red roan horse he was riding, they said. Who said? Her stepdad. Ray Whitfield was an official deputy sheriff and had authority to make arrests. He had locked the boy in the jail and left. According to the old story, the boy had been chained to a bed in Chester Tuttle's cabin, simply because they had no place else to keep him and they couldn't let him just run away. They'd kept him chained to the bed overnight, then had found a way next morning to get him off their hands.

Had they fed him today? She doubted it. All afternoon she sneaked glances at the front of the sheriff's office to see if anyone carried food inside. No one went in and no one came out. Young Waggoner was alone, locked up like a caged animal.

"Do you believe it, Mr. Woodbine?" she asked. "That he stole the horse?"

The merchant shrugged. "Who knows. Way I heard it the horse is wearing a Texas brand. The sheriff can find out when he gets back. He can send a message on the telegraph and find out."

"But Sheriff Rogers won't be back until tomorrow. Maybe not even then."

"Well, he's a drifter, and a few days in the hoosegow won't hurt him. Wonder what he bought that shovel for?"

She knew, but she didn't tell. Instead she said, "He hasn't been fed. I've been watching."

"It takes a man a long time to starve, but, well, you could talk to your dad and see if he'll take him something

21

to eat."

"He's not my dad. My father was Captain Carbaugh of the United States Cavalry."

"I know. Nobody could understand why you wouldn't take your stepdad's name — but me, I'm beginning to understand."

"I appreciate that, Mr. Woodbine."

They closed the store just before sundown, but instead of going straight to her rented two-room cabin as usual, she went to the combination sheriff's office and jail. The outer door was unlocked. She paused a moment, wondering if she was doing the right thing, then opened the door and stepped inside. The sheriff's guns were in a rack on a wall, and the jail key was hanging from a nail under the gun rack. She could unlock the jail door and let him out. But she wouldn't. That would be criminal. Another gun lay on the sheriff's desk, a walnut-handled pistol in a holster. She stepped up to the iron door between the sheriff's office and the jail.

He'd been sitting on the bunk with his head in his hands. His head came up when he heard the outer door open. When he saw who opened it he stood. She spoke to him through the bars in the iron door: "Your name is Waggoner, isn't it?"

"Yeah." There was defiance in his voice.

"Your mother is buried on a bluff east of here. Her name was Matilda Waggoner."

"You know all about me, huh?" Daylight coming through the outer door showed her a pinched angry face. But it was a good face with a smooth clean jawline and a wide firm mouth.

She felt like apologizing for knowing something of his life. "No sir, Mr. Waggoner, I don't know it all. I . . . my mother and I came here after it, uh, it happened. I heard about it, and I saw your mother's grave."

"Yeah, well?" He was still defiant.

"Have you had anything to eat?

"Naw."

22

"I'll bring you something. I'll go home and fix you something to eat."

Snapping the words, he said, "Don't worry about it. I'll live."

"I'll be right back." She turned so fast her long skirt swirled around her ankles, and she went through the door without closing it.

Darn it, she said to herself as she walked with quick steps to her cabin, nobody has any proof that he stole that horse. Nobody has any proof that he ever did anything wrong. He doesn't owe anyone in this county a gosh-darned thing.

In her wood-frame cabin, she built a fire in a cast-iron stove and put a pot of beef stew on to warm. While it warmed, she cut two thick slices from a loaf of bread and put two patties of rich butter on each slice. Then she washed her face in a basin that sat on a small table. In a small alcove off the room was a narrow bed with springs and a mattress. A wire was stretched across one end of the alcove. That was where she hung her clothes. Looking at herself in a mirror on a wall, she wondered whether she looked her best, whether she should change clothes. She wished she'd washed her hair the night before. That was something she was planning to do tonight.

By now the stew was too hot to handle, and she dumped kindling wood out of a small wooden box beside the stove, ladled a plate full of the stew, and put the plate in the box. A knife and fork and the bread went into the box next, and she covered the whole thing with a freshly-washed flour sack.

Let the whole town know what she was doing. They had treated him like an animal once before, and they shouldn't be allowed to do it again. Let them talk. Who cares?

She got back to the jail just before dark. In the pale light that came through the open outer door, his face registered surprise at seeing her. "Here's some stew," she said. "It was the only thing I could fix quick. I cooked it last night and

23

warmed it up just now."

"Well . . ." He took the warm plate when she passed it between the bars. "I sure do thank you, miss." Some of the anger was gone from his face. "But why?"

"Never mind why. Here's some bread. Do you have drinking water? I'll fetch some." Night was coming on fast and she could barely see him now.

He repeated, "I sure do thank you, miss. Carbaugh? Is that what you said your name is?"

"Yes. Janet Carbaugh." She started to leave, then paused. "Uh, Mr. Waggoner, I hope you didn't come here for revenge."

"Why? Why should you care?" He took a bite of the bread.

"I know what happened. It was terrible, what they did to you, and I certainly can't blame you if you're looking for revenge, but I . . . you would only ruin your own life."

He stopped chewing for a moment. He'd heard the same thing from Mrs. Nance and Zack Dawson. He'd heard it so often he believed it. "I can say honestly that I didn't come here to get even with anybody."

"I'm happy to hear that, Mr. Waggoner. I'll fetch a pail of water."

Outside, it was nearly dark, but she had no fear of the dark. As she walked past an alley next to the Prairie Rose saloon she heard men's voices, low, serious. Pausing, she listened. A man said:

"Tie 'im to old Butler's barn and give 'im a few good licks with a bullwhip and he'll be more'n glad to get plumb out of the territory."

She recognized the voice. The man was known only as Case, and he worked for her stepfather.

"Git shut of 'im," another man said.

"Wait till it's good and dark. Won't be no moon tonight."

Oh my gosh. Her heart jumped into her throat. They were going to horsewhip him. She had to do something. Stepping back out of sight of the alley, she tried to think.

24

She remembered the jail key hanging on a wall in the sheriff's office. Oh my gosh, is that why all the doors except the jail door were unlocked? So a mob could get in? And that gun on the sheriff's desk, that had to be his gun, the one he was carrying. Oh my gosh.

Stepping fast, she went back to the sheriff's office and groped with her hands in the dark until she found the gun, then the jail key. "Mr. Waggoner," she said, "you have to get out of here." She couldn't see him in the dark.

"Huh? Why?"

Fumbling, she found the keyhole, inserted the key, and turned it. "There are some men planning to hurt you. Quickly, leave." The door swung open on iron hinges. "Here. I think this is your gun. Please don't shoot anyone."

She felt him rather than saw him step close. His hands grabbed the gun and holster. "Listen, young lady, you could get in serious trouble."

"I don't care. I can't just stand by and let them . . . please hurry."

"All right. I'll go out first. Don't follow until I'm gone, but get out before they come."

She heard his boots clomp to the door, saw him silhouetted for a second in the pale light in the doorway, then saw him slip outside. After a minute, she slipped out herself and started to hurry back to her cabin. Then she heard a man shout: "Hey, is that him? Hey, he's gettin' away."

A fearful whisper came from her throat, "Oh my gosh."

Chapter Six

He broke into a run when he heard the shouts behind him. They wanted to catch him, beat him, maybe hang him. He ran toward the barn where he'd left his horse the night before, but when he got there he knew he didn't have time to find the horse in the dark and saddle him. Squatting, he quickly unbuckled his spurs, left them on the ground, and ran.

"He's over at the barn. Don't let 'im get a horse."

"Is that him? Hey. Hey, stop or I'll shoot." A large-caliber gun popped behind him.

Bending low to make himself as small a target as possible, he ran into the tall grass and weeds that grew along Apache Creek. Another shot was fired.

"Goddamn it, git after 'im."

"I'm runnin' as fast as I can."

Two more shots were fired, but the men were shooting in the dark. He kept on running, his breath coming in gasps. Then he ran into a downed tree, barking his shins painfully, and fell across it. For a moment he lay there, trying to get his wind. His pursuers were coming closer.

"He's in the weeds. Shoot the shit out of 'im."

"Yeah, we got a right to shoot 'im now. He's a jailbreaker."

"You fellers go on. I got to stop and blow awhile."

Bullets whined like angry hornets over his head, thumped the ground beside him, and smacked into the cottonwood log in front of him. He hugged the ground. The log was old and rotten. It wouldn't stop a bullet fired up close. He had to move, but with so many bullets in the air it would be dangerous to move. They were coming closer.

It was just a matter of time until they found him. Though the night was black, sooner or later one of them would stumble over him or the log and find him. What would he do?

He had been carrying the gunbelt and holster in his hands, and when the shooting let up for a few seconds, he got to his knees and buckled the belt around his waist. The old Army .44 was like a friend in his right hand as he waited. He'd shoot, he decided, before he'd just sit here and let them kill him.

Then he realized it was quiet. The gunfire had stopped and the men had stopped running. A man couldn't move much in those weeds without making a sound. Why had they stopped?

A whisper: "Any idee where he's at, Case?"

"He's not far away. Listen. If you hear anything, shoot the shit out of it."

"Don't shoot over this way. I'm over here."

"Wait and listen."

Behind his log, Jim Waggoner tried not to breathe. He had an urge to jump up and run, but that would be suicide. All he could do was wait. And when he thought about it, he could wait as long as they could. He could wait all night, if he had to. At daylight maybe some of the other townspeople would come to see what was going on. Maybe cooler heads would keep him alive.

Maybe.

Cooler heads sure as hell hadn't helped eleven years ago.

Thinking of that made him grind his teeth and grip the butt of the Army Colt a little tighter. All right, you blood-thirsty sons of bitches. Come and find me. You'll pay a hell of a high price for killing me.

There was movement again. Another whisper: "I bet he's right over there. I rec'lect an old blowed-down cotton-wood over there. I bet he's behind it." They were moving. They were coming.

"Hey, somebody's got a lantern. Who is it?"

"Don't know. He's comin' from the barn."

"I bet it's old Butler. Let's borry his light."

"Not me. If that goddamn kid's got a gun, that light'd make a damn fine target."

"Go tell old Butler to put that goddamn light out."

Someone walked away through the weeds. The light went out. "All right," a man whispered, "I think that log's right over to the east a little bit. Be careful. He's prob'ly got a gun."

Jim Waggoner believed he was going to die. All he could do now was kill as many of those sons of bitches as he could before they got him. He hadn't come back to Apache Creek to kill anyone, but it looked like he had no choice. He was ready to kill.

Then the words of old Zack Dawson came to his mind. Old Zack, with a jaw full of snuff, always spitting, always talking. But he was a wise old bird, and some of the things he said made sense. "What good is gettin' even," he'd said one night, "if you git yourself killed doin' it? Gettin' even ain't no satisfaction to a dead man."

He was right. Jim Waggoner didn't want to die. He wanted to get away. How could he do it?

He wondered what was behind him. Was there an ar-royo where the creek ran? If there was, could he get down in it without being shot? They were coming again, moving cautiously. A gun popped, and Jim saw the flash of gunfire.

"It's him." Another pop, then another. Jim cocked the hammer back on the Colt .44, and was glad their shooting covered the ratcheting sound it made.

"Aw, shit, that's just one a them cottontail rabbits."

"The hell it is. It made too much noise for a rabbit."

"Whatever it was, it's full of holes now."

"Reckon it's him?"

"Naw. I bet he's right over there." They were closer.

He thought about firing a shot to stop them, make them afraid to come closer. But if he did they'd shoot so many slugs into that log that one of the slugs would hit him. At least one. Probably a half-dozen.

There was only one thing to do. Move. Fast. Hope for luck. Run for the creek. Gripping the Colt, Jim Waggoner jumped up and ran.

A man yelled, "There he goes." Guns boomed. Muzzles belched lead, fire, and smoke. Slugs hit the ground around him, whined over his head. He put his head down and ran.

The ground dropped from under him and he fell.

Chapter Seven

He'd made a mistake, cocking the hammer on the .44. When he hit the ground on his hands and knees, the hammer tripped, exploding the percussion cap which exploded the black powder which sent a lead ball through the grass ahead.

But he was alive. And he was relieved to be able to move his arms and legs. He was alive and unhurt. Groping with his hands, he reckoned he'd fallen off a bank about four feet high. The sound of running water told him he was beside the creek. And the sound of men's voices told him he couldn't stay there.

Still gripping the gun, he ran east along the creek, stumbling over uneven ground, sticks, and fallen tree limbs. Gunfire came from behind him as he turned and splashed into the creek. There were more shots, but the men were shooting in his general direction without a target to aim at. He stumbled over something in the creek and fell onto his hands and knees again, this time in the water. Now his gun was wet, and he doubted it would fire if he needed it.

Across the creek, he pushed through the tall grass and hogweeds and kept going until he was out on the prairie. There, he turned east again and ran until he thought his lungs were going to burst.

He felt safe now — hidden in an awful lot of dark prairie. The men were still pursuing him, but they had no idea where he was. Still, the farther away he got the safer he was. As soon as his breathing returned to normal, he walked, still heading east, his footsteps making little sound in the short prairie grass.

While he walked, he tried to figure out what he was going to do. He was afoot. When daylight came he would no longer be safe. Men on horseback would find him. Him and his wet gun. All they would have to do was ride up to him and put a rope around his neck. He was a jailbreaker. That made him fair game.

They might even hang him from the same tree they'd hung his dad and Uncle Tobe from. No. No, by God, they might shoot him, but they weren't going to hang him. And if the powder in his gun would dry, he'd take some of them down with him.

Walking on, it occurred to him that he could be near the tree where the double hanging had taken place eleven years ago. He turned his footsteps north until he came to the tall grass. Yeah, he could be near it. In fact, he could be standing on their graves. Pushing through the weeds he could hear water again. He looked up at the sky and could barely see a dim line where the earth ended and the sky began. The stars put out very little light, and the sky was a shade lighter, but only a shade. He walked on east, feeling the tall grass and weeds brush his pants legs. Twice he stepped into depressions in the ground and fell onto his hands and knees. Still, he carried the heavy revolver in his hand rather than have it pulling on his right side.

Something blotted out the sky. A tree. Groping his way to it, he could tell by feel that it was a big tree. A breeze rustled the flat green leaves. It was The Tree. With a groan, he dropped to the ground and sat with his back against it.

The memory. The sight that wouldn't leave his mind. He tried to push it away, but it wouldn't budge. He put his arms across his knees and buried his face in his arms.

Their faces. Black. Eyes nearly out of their sockets. Tongues hanging out. And the blood. Blood running

31

down their chins and onto their shirts. Blood from their tongues. They had bitten their tongues in agony.

There was no scaffolding, no wagon. They had been pulled up with their hands tied behind their backs, pulled up by a dozen pairs of strong arms, and left hanging by their necks until their feet quit kicking and their legs quit twitching and they were dead.

No matter how he tried, Jim Waggoner couldn't forget. Time and willpower had dimmed the memory until he had learned to live with it. But now, sitting under the tree where it had happened, it seemed like only yesterday. Why, he asked himself, had he come back?

The hurt was in him again, and with the hurt came the anger. Anger and frustration. He remembered the frustration he'd felt when he broke away from Mrs. Tuttle and ran as hard as he could run to the tree. Too late. It was over. He remembered trying to climb the tree to cut them down and being grabbed by a dozen hands and carried away. He remembered kicking, hitting, crying, scratching, biting. All for nothing.

"Forget it," Mrs. Nance had said. "You're only hurting yourself. You're young and you've got a lot of living to do. Don't ruin your life by dwelling on bad memories. Read the Good Book and believe in the Lord."

He'd tried. He was still trying. Remember the good things, Mrs. Nance had said. What was Dad like? And Uncle Tobe?

Jonathan and Tobe Waggoner had driven a hundred cows and two bulls from west Texas to what was then Kansas Territory. Uncle Tobe had been there before. He'd tried his hand at placer mining at Auraria, later named Denver. But Uncle Tobe was no miner. He was a farmer and cattleman. And when he made his way back to Texas in the middle of the winter, he was amazed at how plentiful the grass was on the prairie east of Auraria, and how fat the buffalo were.

And the land was free. Well, not yet, but it would be. Sooner or later the U.S. Government would make a deal with the Indians and open it up for sale or homesteading. Whoever had settled on it first would have preemption rights and would get the first chance to buy it or homestead it. "Let's git up there and git some of that country while the gittin's good," Tobe Waggoner had said to his younger brother.

Jonathan's son was nine at the time, big enough to sit a horse and help keep the cattle moving in the right direction. His wife drove the team that pulled their one wagon. She was a slender, pretty young woman who came from good Tennessee stock. Though she was brought up a lady, she could harness and drive the team and cook a meal with nothing more to burn than buffalo chips and dry grass.

They had picked a spot on a curve in Apache Creek and dug a shelter into the side of a bluff. The men did a lot of riding, looking for other sources of water, and when they found none for over twenty miles, they knew they had picked the right spot. The cattle gained weight, and Jonathan praised his brother for recognizing good year-round grass when he saw it.

And Mrs. Waggoner. She had always kept a cheerful face while living in a one-room dugout, rustling firewood and learning to butcher and cook wild meat. She kept herself and her son clean, and made him practice his reading and arithmetic. She taught him good manners. Her son would be a gentleman, she vowed.

It was a hard life, but the brothers had plans. They would sell beef to the gold hunters over west, buy more land, bring more cattle up from Texas and build a cattle empire. Mrs. Waggoner shared in their enthusiasm. In a few years life would be good . . .

Yep, young Jim Waggoner said to himself, those are the things I ought to be remembering. The good things.

But how in hell — excuse me, Mrs. Nance — how in all that's holy am I going to get out of this fix?

He was in a fix, all right. When daylight came, men on horseback would be looking for him, a jailbreaker. He wouldn't be hard to find. The only hiding place in twenty miles was along the creek, and that is where they'd look. With wet powder in his gun, he wouldn't even be able to put up a fight.

Maybe the powder would dry. Naw, not at night. And his powder flask, lead balls, and percussion caps were in his saddlebags back in town. If he could leave the gun in the sun, the powder would dry in an hour or so. Maybe. No way to be sure except to try it. If they didn't find him until an hour or more after sunup, he might get a shot at some of them.

But he couldn't shoot them all. And if he shot any of them, they would use that as an excuse to hang him.

He couldn't help feeling a little sarcastic when he thought, All right, Mrs. Nance, look in your Good Book and tell me what to do.

That was when it occurred to him that there was only one thing to do. Yeah, the more he thought about it, the more he liked the idea. The territory was divided into counties and had laws and lawmen. It had courts. He had committed no crime. A bill of sale for the red roan horse was in his saddlebags. The law was supposed to protect the innocent. Let it protect him.

Jim Waggoner stood and started walking again. He walked out to the wagon road, and kept going in the dark. He walked back to town.

Chapter Eight

With his hat for a pillow, the wooden bunk in the jail cell wasn't too uncomfortable. Jim Waggoner had spent many nights in worse places. What worried him most was the dark. As long as the outer door and the cell door were closed he had no way of knowing when daylight came. He slept, got up and walked the floor, lay down and slept some more. He was lying on the bunk with his hands under his head when he heard the train whistle.

The steam whistle started screaming long before the train puffed, hissed, and screeched its way into town. Jim had seen a train once. It was something to see. The big steam engine had more power than a dozen horses. More than two or three dozen. And it never tired. The train crew had to stop once in a while to load up with water and fuel, but that didn't take long, and the engine was ready to go again, hissing and blowing smoke like a huge animal.

Wherever the trains were, life was different. For most folks, life was better. And the land, the land was more expensive. The U.S. government gave land to the railroad builders to help them raise the needed money. The railroads sold the land for more money than government land cost. But it was worth more. Land near a railroad where cattle, crops, and other products could be shipped was valuable.

He listened. Peering between the bars of the iron door, he could see pale daylight shining under the outer door.

35

Men would be looking for him now, riding down the creek, across every draw. One of the places they'd look was the dugout on Apache Creek. They'd have guns in their hands ready to shoot. And—he chuckled to himself—all the time he was right here in town.

Not long after the train came in, he heard the outer door open. Standing, peering through the bars, he saw a man enter and leave the door open. Not knowing at first who the man was, he backed into a corner of the cell, near the door, where he couldn't be seen from the office. Then, when no footsteps came to the door, he carefully peered between the bars again. The man was in his forties, a little stout, with gray bushy eyebrows and gray hair showing under a gray wide-brim hat. He carried a pistol in a holster high on his right side, and he had a silver star pinned to a pocket on his shirt.

Without looking at the iron door, the sheriff opened his desk, put something in it, and started to leave. He stopped and spun around suddenly when Jim Waggoner kicked the cell door.

"Huh?" The sheriff's face was round and well-fed. Smooth-shaven. "What? Who's there? Is somebody in there?"

He drew his gun and approached the cell like he was walking up to a bear. "Who's in there?"

Jim didn't answer, just stood back away from the door with his hands on his hips.

"Who the hell are you? What're you doing in there?" The sheriff's deep-set eyes took in the Army Colt in its holster. "Who locked you in there?"

Still, Jim didn't answer. Not until the sheriff's eyes went to the nail on the wall where the cell key was usually kept did he speak. "Looking for this?" Jim held the key on its ring up to the bars in the door.

"What's going on here? How come you locked yourself in?"

"It's the safest place." He reached between the bars and unlocked the door himself.

As the door swung open, the lawman looked Jim over carefully, holstered his gun, and said, "I don't know who you are, young feller, but you've got some explaining to do."

"Be happy to, sheriff."

Janet Carbaugh had seen the men riding out of town early in the morning, all carrying rifles, and she knew who they were after. Now she watched Sheriff Thomas J. Rogers walk along the plankwalk to his combination office and jail. She wanted to hurry over to the sheriff and tell him what had happened. But she couldn't get rid of Mrs. Tuttle.

"Oh, and yes, I need some white thread, Janet, if you've got some. And better add a spool of blue thread too. Good heavy thread, not that flimsy stuff. Now that Mr. Tuttle is serving in the General Assembly and spending most of his time in Denver, he wears mostly store-bought clothes, but I make my own dresses, as you know, and I think I'll make a pretty one out of white and blue calico with some of that lacy trim. When you get in some more of that ready-made trim, give me a holler, will you?"

Janet almost ran, gathering the goods, placing them on the long wooden counter, adding the price of each item. Glancing through the big glass window, she saw Sheriff Rogers leave his office and walk toward Ma Baker's cafe. She had a terrible urge to catch him and try to persuade him to go after those men before it was too late.

"On second thought, Janet, I think I'll make Mr. Tuttle a shirt out of whatever is left of the calico. Even if he does have to dress like a gentleman while he's at the Capitol, he needs a good everyday shirt when he's at home. What kind of buttons have you got now?"

"Yes, Mrs. Tuttle. Uh, Mrs. Tuttle, could I, uh, would you excuse me for a minute? Just for a minute. I need to talk to Sheriff Rogers and I see him across the street. Just for a minute, Mrs. Tuttle."

"Why, Janet, what in the name of Job is the matter? What—" But Janet was out the door.

As she ran, Janet had to hold her long skirts above her shoes with both hands to keep from tripping. She caught the sheriff just as he was about to open the door to Ma Baker's cafe. "Sheriff. Sheriff Rogers. One moment, please."

The lawman stopped. "Miss Carbaugh? Something wrong?"

"Yes, Sheriff, there is." Speaking rapidly, she told him all about it. But instead of hurrying to the barn for a horse, Sheriff Rogers just hooked his thumbs in his gunbelt and smiled. "Now don't you worry none, Miss Carbaugh. That young feller is safe and sound."

"What? How? I don't understand."

Still grinning, the lawman said, "He's no dummy, that boy. He done exactly the right thing. While old Case and them are riding all over the county lookin' for him, he's locked himself up in my jail."

Dumbfounded, Janet said, "He did?"

"Yup. Done exactly the right thing. Locked himself up and kept the key in the jail with him. If they wanted to whip him or hang him or anything, they'd have to bust in the jail to get to him." The smile turned into a chuckle. "Ever hear of such a thing, Miss Carbaugh? Busting into a jail? And if they'd poked a gun barrel between the bars and shot him, I'd be locking them up for murder."

A long sigh of relief came out of Janet Carbaugh. "Thank goodness."

Squinting at her, Sheriff Rogers said, "Do you know that feller, Miss? Said his name is James Waggoner. Seems to me I heard that name before."

"Yes. No. I mean I know of him." Glancing back at the store across the street, she added, "Sheriff, it's a long story, and I was waiting on Mrs. Tuttle. I have to get back. When you finish your breakfast I'll be happy to tell you what I know."

"A long story, eh?"

"Yes. You've probably heard it. Meanwhile, is he still locked up? Has he had any breakfast?"

"Yeah. Since my special deputy arrested him I don't think I ought to turn him out until my deputy tells me himself about it. And no, but I'm fixing to take him somethin' to eat."

"Good. I'll be at the store."

A few minutes later, Mrs. Tuttle said, "I don't know what's got you so flustered, Janet. You've always attended to business before. Has it got something to do with that young man that broke out of jail last night?"

"As a matter of fact, Mrs. Tuttle, it has."

"You know who he is, don't you?"

"Yes. I know. You told me about him yourself."

"Well, at the time I told you about him I didn't expect to ever see him again." Mrs. Tuttle's eyes narrowed in her usually pleasant face and her voice took on a worried note. "I hope he's not here for revenge. His pa and uncle got a fair trial. Mr. Tuttle was the land club's judge as well as the land recorder. Lord knows there was no other law here then, and we had to have some way to settle differences."

"Yes, I know. You all did the best you could. Only . . . some people think the punishment was too severe."

The older woman's face was set in hard lines now. "You came along later, and you don't know what it was like. There were land grabbers and horse thieves and cattle thieves, so many that it was hard to keep anything from being stolen. And we had no jail then. The criminals had to be sentenced immediately and the sentence had to be carried out immediately."

"I suppose. But it was awfully hard on that boy."

Finally, Mrs. Tuttle softened. "It was, I admit, with his ma already dead and no other kin that we knew of. But we did the best we could for him. We found him a good

39

home." The eyes squinted again. "You talked to him, didn't you, Janet? Is he here for revenge?"

"I don't really know, Mrs. Tuttle, but somehow I don't think that's why he's here. I think he only . . . well, I just don't know."

"Well." Mrs. Tuttle gathered her purchases and turned to leave. "I only hope he goes away before someone gets killed."

Janet watched her go through the screen door, and spoke aloud to herself, "That would be nice, wouldn't it, Mrs. Tuttle, if he would just quietly go away."

But Janet worried that although James Waggoner might have come to Apache Wells with peaceful intentions, the way he was treated last night could change his attitude.

People could be killed.

Chapter Nine

By the time Sheriff Rogers came back for the dirty breakfast dishes, the sun was high and it was hotter in the jail cell than the hinges of hell. Ray Whitfield was with him. Two gray men.

"All right, now, young feller, you say you got a bill of sale for the horse you was riding, is that right?"

"Yeah, Sheriff, it's in my saddlebags."

"And Ray here tells me they took the horse and saddle and all over to Butler's barn. Is that right, Ray?"

"Right as rain. If he can't pay for the keep, old Butler can sell his saddle. Bet he stole the saddle too."

Sheriff Rogers drew his pistol and unlocked the iron door. "All right, Waggoner, we'll just go over to the barn and have a looksee. If you can produce a bill of sale, I'll put this here gun away and you can go on about your business. What is your business, anyway? Did you come here with the idea of getting even with somebody?"

Jim Waggoner stepped out of the cell, pushed his hat back and wiped sweat from his forehead with a shirtsleeve. "That ain't why I came back, but . . ." He locked eyes with Ray Whitfield. "You remember me, Mr. Whitfield, and I damn well remember you."

"What the hell is that supposed to mean?" Whitfield put a hand on his gun butt.

"Yeah, young feller," the lawman said, "if you got any

41

intention of starting trouble, you just remember how hot it is in that there jail."

"Where's my money and my gun?"

"I don't know nothin' about no money, and your gun is in my desk. I'll give it to you as soon as you show me a bill of sale."

"They took over two hundred dollars out of my pocket. They pointed guns at me and took my money. If they say they didn't, then they're nothing but thieves."

Turning his head toward Whitfield, the sheriff asked, "Did he have any money?"

"None that I saw."

"You saw it, all right," Jim said.

Whitfield stepped in front of him. "Are you calling me a liar?"

"If that money doesn't turn up, then yeah, you're a liar."

"Now look here," Sheriff Rogers put in, "we're not going to have a fight here and now. First thing we'll do is have a look at that bill of sale then figure out where to go from there."

They walked to the barn, Jim in the lead, followed by the sheriff and Ray Whitfield. The sheriff holstered his pistol, but warned, "If you try to jackrabbit, I'll shoot to kill."

At the barn, Jim saw his red roan gelding in a pen with three other horses. Scraps of grass hay led him to believe the horses had been fed. Inside the barn, four saddles straddled a horizontal pole against a wall. Jim walked up to his saddle, opened the deep leather pockets tied behind the cantle, and groped through them. He took out the one change of clothes he had, the powder flask, percussion caps, and lead balls. That was all there was.

With hatred in his eyes he turned to Ray Whitfield. "You stole it. Just like you stole my money. I had a bill of sale signed by George Walls, the manager of the Double O in west Texas. I worked for that horse, and by god he belongs to me."

Instead of facing him, Whitfield turned away and said

42

over his shoulder, "There you have it, Tom. I told you he's a thief."

Cold rage swept over Jim. With two long steps he caught Whitfield from behind, grabbed him by the neck, and slammed him against a wooden box stall. "You lying son of a bitch. You stole my money and you stole my bill of sale. You goddamn lying son of a bitch." His left fist punched into the older man's middle and his right fist thudded against the left temple.

Whitfield's eyes crossed and he went down in a heap on the barn floor, nearly unconscious. Jim bent over to grab the gun on Whitfield's right hip. A sharp red pain cracked against the side of his head and he collapsed on top of Whitfield.

He was stretched out on the cool dirt floor of the barn, and when he opened his eyes he saw the peaked barn roof and two-by-six rafters. Someone or something was pounding on the right side of his head. His arm, when he tried to move it, felt like lead.

"You awake, boy?"

It took some straining, but he managed to move his eyeballs far enough to see Sheriff Rogers squatting beside him, holding a long-barreled pistol. Someone else was behind the sheriff. Who? Oh, Butler, the man who owned the barn. Forcing his eyeballs to rove, Jim looked for Whitfield. Didn't see him.

"If you ain't dead, son, get up."

Grunting, straining, Jim raised to a sitting position, fell back, raised up again. His vision swam, and he tried to remember what had happened. The gun in the sheriff's hand told him what had happened. He'd been pistol whipped. Knocked out. "Oh," he grunted, trying to get to his feet.

"You're going back to jail, son, and we ain't about to carry you, so stand up and walk."

"Uh." Slowly, painfully, feeling like he was going to fall again, Jim stood. He swayed like a drunken man, and leaned against a stall door for support.

43

"He owes me for keepin' that horse." It was Butler, the barn owner, talking.

"Well, if the horse ain't stolen and he can't pay, you got a right to sell the horse and take what he owes you out of the proceeds."

"Yeah," Butler replied sourly. "If he ain't stole."

"There's ways of finding out. Now, young feller, start walking."

Jim walked. Wobbly. Once he stumbled and almost fell, but gathered himself and kept his feet moving. As he walked, his head cleared and he began to think. "You said, Sheriff, there are other ways of finding out about that horse."

"Yeah, we got a telegraph wire. I can send a message to Denver and they can wire it to wherever I want it to go."

"There's no telegraph wire at Pretty Prairie, Texas."

"Well, I can send a message to the telegraph station closest to there and somebody can carry it the rest of the way. That is, if you're sure you want me to send a message. If I do and it don't prove you own that horse, it'll just add to your jail time."

"Send a message to George Walls at Pretty Prairie, Texas. Everybody in west Texas knows who he is."

It had been at the Double O headquarters a year ago when Jim Waggoner had first seen the red roan. His personal horse was getting up in years, and the young man had been looking for a trade. George Walls offered him a deal.

"You break ten head of these four-year-olds, James, and break them so they're dependable mounts, and I'll give you a fair wage and the roan colt. How's that?"

"That'll be fine, Mr. Walls. That is, if you'll retire that old bay horse of mine."

Lord, it was hot in the jail.

Thinking of the Double O reminded him of Charlie and Mrs. Nance. He'd been hired in Pretty Prairie at age thirteen, a ragged, homeless drifter, and taken in a two-horse buggy to a house and some pens on the north fork of

44

Adobe Creek. There he lived with the Nances and helped with the work on that end of the Double O holdings. Charlie Nance was a hired hand himself, but for over two years he was the boy's boss. It was Mrs. Nance, though, he would never forget.

She was a religious woman, who bowed her head and gave thanks before every meal. The boy was used to that after living in the Colony for a year. But Charlie Nance sometimes grumbled something about how it wasn't the Lord who provided. "It's strong hands and backs and hosses," he'd said. "It's them hosses we oughta be givin' thanks to."

Mrs. Nance had seen that the boy was troubled. He never smiled, and his face was always pinched. The first year he'd stayed with them he refused to talk much. But with patience and kindness she eventually got him to tell about it.

"Oh good heavens," she had said. "No wonder you're troubled. I'll pray for you, and you must pray too. Remember what Jesus said? He said, 'Forgive them their sins, Father, for they know not what they do.' You must forgive too, James. You're young and healthy and intelligent. Don't ruin your life by hating somebody."

Then one day Charlie Nance had tried to say something funny, and the boy smiled. Charlie had put a hand on his shoulder and said, "You're a good worker, Jimmie, and gettin' to be a good hand with young horses. But don't be so dod-damned serious all the time." He thought if he pronounced the word as "dod," he wasn't using God's name in vain.

Thinking about it, Jim had to smile again. But in the suffocating heat of the jail, the smile slipped. He realized he was on the verge of hating again. He'd lost his temper and exploded. What did it get him? A pistol barrel upside the head and a hotbox of a jail. And he'd be here a while.

At least he had water. Sheriff Rogers had brought a bucket of clear water and a tin cup. He wouldn't die of dehydration. But, dammit, a man could barely breathe in here, and he didn't like being locked up and . . .

Jim Waggoner sat on the bunk, feeling the old bitterness rise inside him.

Chapter Ten

It was hot inside Janet Carbaugh's rented two-room house too. Even with a window open, she was uncomfortable. She wished there were more windows so a cross breeze could flow through the house, but the builder had been more concerned with keeping out the winter winds. Janet lay on top of the bed linens in a thin nightdress and worried about the young man in the county jail.

It would take several days to get a message back from somewhere in Texas, a message that would prove James Waggoner was innocent. Meanwhile, he was suffering in jail. It wasn't right. It wasn't justice. In spite of all the laws and courts and officers of the law, there was still a lot of injustice. She had to help him.

Next morning she was waiting on the plankwalk in front of the sheriff's office when he showed up and unlocked the door.

"Morning, Miss Carbaugh. Do you want something?"

"Yes, Mr. Rogers, I would like to talk to you."

"Come on inside and sit."

She followed him inside. The young man's face appeared briefly between the bars in the iron door. She sat in a wooden chair beside the sheriff's desk, keeping her back to the jail. The face, in the glimpse she'd had of it, was the face of a caged animal, and she couldn't stand to look at it. Before the sheriff could say anything, she began:

"He's entitled to bail, you know. The law provides that.

And besides, under the law the accused doesn't have to prove his innocence, the accuser has to prove his guilt. That hasn't been done. And if there were a courthouse here and a full-time judge, I'm sure the judge would order the prisoner released, and—"

"Whoa now. Hold on, here. Where did you learn all this, in that school in Denver?" Sheriff Rogers dropped into the only other chair in the room.

"Yes. We have studied modern civilization, and now that Colorado is a Territory of the United States, we are supposed to be civilized, and we are not supposed to lock men up on vague suspicions. Furthermore, the United States Constitution says there shall be no cruel or unusual punishment, and locking men inside that suffocating jail is cruel and unusual. What's more, if I have to go to Denver and get a writ from the judge, that's what I'll do, and I'll do it immediately."

"A writ? A writ, you say? One of those habeas corpus things?"

"Exactly. I've never seen one, but I know what it is: it's a note from the judge ordering you to release the prisoner."

"Well, now." Sheriff Rogers studied the floor a moment. "If he had any money, enough to pay for the horse, I'd let him post it for bail. But I'd keep the horse till he could prove he owns him. That way, if he quit the country, we'd at least have the horse."

"He has no money?"

"Not a cent."

"Well, I have. How much is bail?"

"Well, now, I'll have to think about that." The sheriff's eyes narrowed. "What's your interest in this, Miss Carbaugh? You're not feeling sorry for that boy, are you?"

"Why, I . . ." She decided not to answer the question. "How much?"

"Oh, say a hundred dollars."

"You know that horse isn't worth that much. There isn't a horse in Apache County worth a hundred dollars."

"All right, fifty."

"I'll get the money."

"You know what'll happen, don't you? If he quits the country I'll have to keep your money. And you can bet that once he gets out of here he'll run so fast you'll think his shirttail's on fire. And where are you gonna get the money? From your dad?"

"From who?"

"Your dad, Ray Whitfield. He won't shell out a cent to get this boy out of jail. You heard how he was attacked, haven't you?"

"Mr. Whitfield is not my father, and yes, I've heard. Everyone has heard."

"And you still want to bail him out?"

"Yes. I'll get the money and I'll be back."

She had to report for work and ask Mr. Woodbine for a few minutes off before she could go to her rented house and get the money. She had one hundred and twenty-five dollars in a jar behind a flour sack on a kitchen shelf. It was all she had left from the sale of twenty-two beeves last fall. The sale had financed two more semesters at the preparatory school in Denver before it closed for the summer. When it closed, she had come back to Apache Wells, but she had stayed at the ranch only a few days before renting a house in town and working for Mr. Woodbine at the mercantile.

It wasn't that her stepfather had mistreated her. In fact he'd always been good to her.

When Janet was sixteen and made it known that she wanted to go to school in Denver, her stepfather had given her ten cows and told her that if she took care of them they would pay her way through school. Take care of them, she did. She was out riding almost every day, seeing that her cattle grazed where the grass was good, and had their illnesses treated. As far as the cowboys were concerned, she was a princess. They even earmarked her cattle with an underslope so she could tell at a glance which were hers. No one ever swore in her presence, though she had heard them use vile language when they didn't know she was

49

near. The only one of the hired hands she didn't like was Case. He was mean to horses and to men. Good men had quit because of Case. But for some reason she didn't understand, her stepfather kept Case around.

The cows had calves, and the calves grew and had calves. Not until she had a herd of twenty-five cows and twenty-two long yearling beeves did she send any to the market in Denver.

No, Ray Whitfield had treated her and her mother well. But after Mrs. Whitfield died, things had begun to change. First it was Mrs. Ramos, the cook. She quit. Whitfield hired a man to do the cooking. The hired men had always eaten in the main house with the family, but they were polite and they ate quickly and quietly. The new cook was a dirty, bottle-sucking old coot named Poco who, though respectful to her, tried to run the house. Janet was the only human female on the ranch, a situation that was making her more and more uncomfortable.

Though she liked the out-of-doors, horses, and cattle, school in Denver was a welcome change.

Half-running, she went back to the sheriff's office. He was gone, but she found him at Ma Baker's cafe eating hotcakes and fried ham. "Here." She handed him the fifty dollars, folded. "This should take care of it."

Back at the store, Mr. Woodbine said, "You're a busy young lady, Janet. You got back just in time to run the store while I go over to the depot and collect the mail and my latest shipment. We've got to have something to sell." He was smiling when he said it.

Janet waited on four customers, stocked some shelves, and was wrestling a keg of tenpenny nails into a corner when Raymond Whitfield came in.

"Morning, Janet."

"Good morning, Mr. Whitfield."

Grinning sheepishly, he said, "If you can't call me Pop, you can at least call me Ray. We lived in the same house for a good many years, you know."

"Yes. You're right. I owe you a lot."

"Naw. Naw, you don't. Just give me a smile now and then."

She forced a smile. "I will, I promise."

"I heard about you putting up bond for the Waggoner boy. How come you did that, Janet?"

"He's . . . oh, I just feel that he's being treated unjustly."

"He didn't have a bill of sale."

"No, he claims it was stolen out of his saddlebags. And he said some money was stolen too."

Whitfield scratched his jaw. He was clean-shaven except for the bushy mustache over a thin-lipped mouth. "About that money. I didn't see any money. I was opening the jail door, I guess, and if there was any money I didn't see it. Last night I asked Case about it, and a couple of other men, and they said they didn't see any money either, but . . ." He stopped talking as if he didn't know what to say next.

Janet's eyebrows went up. "But?"

"Well, you know, hired hands come and go and a couple of them fellers ain't worked for me very long, and I, uh — aw, dammit, I don't know anything about any money. You believe me, don't you, Janet?"

She studied his face a moment. "Yes. I believe you."

The sheepish grin returned. "I'm mighty glad to hear you say that. I — "

Before he could finish what he'd started to say, the screen door opened and two women came in. "Morning, ladies," Whitfield said, touching his hat brim. To Janet he said, "I'll be seeing you."

When she had a moment, Janet looked out the window at the sheriff's office across the street and down the block. She wondered if young Waggoner had been released yet. She worried about what he would do next. She didn't even think about the fifty dollars.

Chapter Eleven

The sun was halfway up in a yellow prairie sky when Jim Waggoner stepped outside onto the plank sidewalk. It was a hot day, but the air felt cool and clean after a night in jail. He'd been fed a breakfast of hotcakes and luke-warm coffee, and he wasn't hungry. But boy, was he dirty. He knew he stank with sweat, and he knew his face was streaked with it. What to do now? He'd left his razor, soap, and a towel at Mrs. Jamison's where he'd stayed one night before spending the next two nights in jail. Would she let him clean up there? He didn't have a cent to pay her. But come to think of it, he'd paid her for two nights' bed and board, believing he'd stay two days before moving on. But Mrs. Jamison was a kind of prissy old gal, and if he showed up looking like this she probably wouldn't let him in.

The town was quiet. Only one buggy went past on the street. Two woman came out of the mercantile and walked down the street in the opposite direction. Mrs. Jamison might not let him in anyway, now that he'd been in jail.

Well, the first thing to do was to get cleaned up. Shifting the .44 and its holster to a more familiar position on his right hip, he headed for Butler's barn to get his saddle-bags.

"The shur'ff tolé me not to let you have your horse," Butler said, mopping his face with a black bandanna. He wore bib overalls with suspenders and a billed cap. His face was freshly shaved, and the smell of bay rum overcame the smell of the barn.

"Yeah, I know," Jim said sourly. "All I want right now is my saddlebags."

"I ain't so sure I should let you have them either. If that horse was stole, I can't keep 'im, and I'll have to keep your saddle till you pay me."

"The saddle ain't worth a damn to me without a horse," Jim said, "but I'm going to take those saddlebags." He walked past Butler to the saddles and unlaced the leather pockets from behind the cantle of his saddle. Butler watched him, but made no move to stop him.

With the saddlebags slung over one shoulder, Jim walked toward the creek, stepping over the downed tree he'd once taken refuge behind in the dark. He pushed his way through the thistles and weeds, climbed down the low bluff he'd once fallen from, and knelt beside the water. After a long look around to be sure no one was in sight, he took off his shirt and hat and splashed water over his face and shoulders and under his armpits. The shirt and cotton pants he took out of the leather bags were wrinkled, and he shook them to get some of the wrinkles out. Then, after another long look around, he pulled off his boots and pants and hastily put on the clean clothes.

His mouth was dry, but he didn't drink. Instead, he recalled words of advice from Charlie Nance: "Afore you take a drink out of a crik better have a look upstream. No tellin' what you'll find in the water."

Maybe Mrs. Jamison would let him have a drink of water if nothing else. He climbed the bank and directed his steps toward Mrs. Jamison's two-story frame house. He sure hoped she was friendly.

She wasn't, and she was.

"Why didn't you tell me who you are?" She stood in the doorway, a tall thin woman with hair that was surprisingly black for a woman in her late fifties.

"I told you my name, remember?" He stood on the

53

porch, the .44 on his hip.

"Yes, you did, but I didn't connect you to . . . well, if you came back here to get revenge on somebody you're too late. Like I told you, my Joe passed away two years ago."

He sighed. "I can honestly say I didn't come here to get revenge."

"Well, my Joe was on that jury, you know."

"I didn't know. I don't remember who all was on the jury."

"Well." The tightness around her mouth relaxed a little. "He always felt kinda bad about it. He never was sure they done the right thing. And me, I thought about you, bein' just a boy with no folks or anything, and bein' sent off with those holy rollers or whatever they was."

"Mrs. Jamison, I need a place to stay, and I did pay you for two nights' board."

"Why are you carryin' that gun?"

"Everybody carries a gun. Every man."

"Well, if you'll take that gun off, you can come in."

He unbuckled the gunbelt and held the gun and holster in his hand. She stepped back out of the doorway.

"Have you had anything to eat today?"

"I can't pay you any more than I've already paid. Somebody stole my money at the jail."

"Set down at the kitchen table anyway. You can pay me when you can, and if you can't, well, I'll know I done somethin' to help you. I heard about you bein' locked up in the jail, and I hope that don't make you mad enough to shoot somebody."

"I'm not happy about it, Mrs. Jamison, but I'm not ready to start a shooting match. I'll tell you this much, though, I intend to try to get my money back."

"You sound like trouble and I don't know if I want you stayin' in my house. But seein' as how you was treated so bad when you was a boy, you can stay. Unless there's trouble."

"All I can say is I didn't come here to start trouble."

She repeated, "Have you had anything to eat today?"

"Yes, ma'am. I'd sure like to shave, though."

"Well, you can go ahead and shave, and I'll cook you some breakfast if you want."

"I appreciate it, but not now."

He went up to the room he'd slept in before, shaved out of a tin washbasin, and combed his hair. Mrs. Jamison left him alone while he did that, but as soon as he finished wiping his face dry and buttoning his shirt, she came into the room and resumed talking.

"My Joe was a good man that wouldn't hurt anybody if he could help it. I don't like to remind you, but your pa and your uncle were tried and convicted of cattle stealin', and —" She shut up when she saw the scowl on his face.

He snapped, "They didn't steal anything. They didn't know where those bulls came from. They didn't brand them until they'd grazed with our cows for over a year."

"Well . . ." The woman was uncertain of herself now. "That was a long time ago. My Joe was a good man. He sold his land claim and worked for the railroad for two years as a labor boss, and when the railroad got to Denver he built this house and then got bit by a rattlesnake and died."

Jim's face was still flushed with anger, but finally he let it die, and shrugged. "You know, I can't even remember your husband. There are only a couple of men I can remember. You say your husband sold his claim?"

"Yes. To Mr. Whitfield."

"Ray Whitfield is one I do remember. He must be the biggest land owner in these parts now."

"He is. He made a lot of money sellin' beef to the railroad to feed the workers, and he bought land all around here."

"I remember him and I remember Chester Tuttle. What's he doing now?"

"Mr. Tuttle went back to Washington for a while. He was there before, you know, tryin' to get the Congress to make this country a legal territory. Now he's elected to the

55

legislature and spends most of his time in Denver."

"Oh?"

"A long time ago him and some others tried to declare this country Jefferson Territory, you know, but the Congress wouldn't allow it."

"Yeah, I read about that in a newspaper."

"So Mr. Tuttle and some others kept tryin', and they finally got President Buchanan to sign the papers. Only they named it Colorado Territory. Some people wanted Chester Tuttle appointed governor, but the president didn't do it. So he got elected to the legislature. Now he spends most of his time in Denver while Mrs. Tuttle stays by herself in their house."

"So Chester Tuttle ain't here much, but Mrs. Tuttle is still here?"

"Yes. She's a harmless soul. You can't be mad at her."

"Naw, I only barely remember her and her husband. I never did know much about any of them. And they wouldn't let me watch the trial."

"I didn't watch it either, but my Joe told me all about it, and he told me about you. He felt real bad about leavin' you with no family." She sat in the one chair in the room and looked at the floor for a moment. "Was it just terrible? What kind of people were those holy rollers?"

"They weren't bad people. They treated me all right."

"I heard they started a colony somewhere around Denver."

"Yeah. It didn't last. Oh, Mrs. Jamison, I've got to go out and try to get my money back. Right now I don't have a cent."

Her head came up. "What are you gonna do?"

"I don't know. Now that I'm cleaned up a little and feeling better, maybe I'll go talk to the sheriff again. See if he can do anything."

"Sheriff Rogers is a good man. Ever'body says he's honest."

"I paid you for two nights' board, but that was three nights ago, and I'll understand if you don't want to cook

56

another meal for me."

Standing, she said, "It's all right. I'll have supper at eight o'clock. That is, if you'll be here."

"I'm planning on it."

Before he hunted up the sheriff, Jim had a chore to take care of. He wished he didn't have to do it, but he did. He walked to the Apache Wells Mercantile, climbed the two steps to the porch, and opened the screen door. Her brown eyes widened when he stepped inside. He hadn't noticed it before, but she was a small young woman, not more than five two, and slender. Her dark hair, parted on the left side, hung down to her shoulders with a curl at the bottom. Another thick dark curl covered the right side of her forehead. She spoke first:

"Good morning, Mr. Waggoner. Or is it afternoon?"

Embarrassed at what he had to say, he stuttered, "I, uh, it must be close to afternoon, Miss Carbaugh. I, uh, I came to thank you. I'll stick around until the sheriff gets an answer to his message. That way you, uh, you'll be sure to get your money back. It was real nice of you, putting up bail money."

The dark hair was soft and feminine. The brown eyes were soft. "I'm sure you're innocent, Mr. Waggoner."

The store owner was seated down the counter, writing in one of his account books. He looked up and studied Jim from his scarred boots to the .44 on his hip to the straw-colored hair and curl-brim hat. He remarked, "You don't seem to be worried about what the answer will be."

"Not if the message gets to Mr. Walls."

"It will. If they don't have a telegraph down there, it'll take a few days, maybe, but the message will get there."

"What are you going to do until then, Mr. Waggoner?"

"Jim. Or James." He grinned a lopsided grin. "I'm not used to being called Mister. And I don't know. Killing time is something else I'm not used to."

"Are you staying at Mrs. Jamison's?"

The lopsided grin remained. "I think so. She hasn't

57

thrown me out yet." The girl wanted to talk, he could tell, but he didn't want to answer any more questions, and he was still embarrassed at having to thank her. "I've got to see the sheriff again, Miss Carbaugh. Please excuse me." Before she could answer, he was on his way out the door.

Whew. That chore was done. He'd be sure she got her money back, and if he could, he'd add some interest. Sure was good of her. Why did she do it? She hadn't been here eleven years ago, had she? He tried to recall a girl about his age, and couldn't. No, she must have come along later. Why should she care about him?

Well, as Mrs. Nance had said, for every bad person in the world there were two or three good ones. He sure hoped he could repay Janet Carbaugh.

That reminded him. There were a lot of thieves in the world too, and some of them stole his money. And while he was walking down the street thinking about it, two of the men who had helped arrest him rode up to the Prairie Rose saloon, dismounted, tied their horses to a hitchrail, and went inside.

Jim had already decided he'd try to get his money back. Right there was a good place to start.

Chapter Twelve

The Prairie Rose saloon was like many others Jim had been in — a long wooden bar with a brass rail and spittoons. A row of whiskey bottles stood on a shelf behind the bar. Pictures of near-naked ladies hung over the whiskey bottles. There were four tables with chairs in the rear of the room. The bartender was short and fat, wearing a striped shirt with no collar and sleeves rolled up past his elbows. His arms were almost as big as Jim's thighs. Two men stood at the bar and four others sat at a table in the rear. One of those at the table was Butler, who owned the barn and corrals where Jim's horse was. All heads turned Jim's way when he stepped inside.

He paused a couple of seconds to let his eyes get accustomed to the dim light, then stepped up to the bigger one of the two, a lantern-jawed man with wide shoulders and hips and a short-barreled pistol in a cutaway holster. Jim didn't know what to say or do. He had no plan. The lantern-jawed man looked him up and down and dared him with his eyes to do anything. Finally, Jim blurted:

"Somebody stole my money. You're the one took it out of my pocket. What did you do with it?"

"The hell you beller. You didn't have no money."

"I had two hundred and ten dollars. One of you stole it."

"Look here, mister." The bartender had his thick arms folded on top of the bar. "If you came in here lookin' to start a fight, you can just git on out of here."

Without looking at him, Jim said, "I came here to get my money back or find out who's got it."

The second man at the bar had a short beard that looked like it had been trimmed with sheep shears. He said, "Best thing you can do, Case, is plug 'im and git rid of 'im."

"Yeah." Case's eyes went to the Colt on Jim's right hip. It was a heavy long-barreled gun, not made for a fast draw. He spoke out of the side of his mouth, "He come in here to start a fight. You all heered 'im. He's accusin' me of stealin' his money. I can't let 'im git by with that, now, can I?" His right hand hovered over the butt of the sixgun.

"You stole it, all right."

"You callin' me a thief?"

Here it was. Jim had been warned that this would happen. It was Zack Dawson who'd sold him the Army Colt and showed him how to use it. That was back when Jim still had half a mind to go up to Colorado and shoot somebody, and he'd practiced with it every day. "You got a natural talent for fast drawin' and shootin'," old Zack had said, "but men that's good with a gun gen'ly go around lookin' to use it and hardly none of 'em lives to old age. Wish I hadn't a sold you that gun."

The air inside the Prairie Rose saloon was hot and tense. Nobody moved. Nobody spoke. Jim locked eyes with Case, but in his mind he was concentrating on the gun and his gun hand. When he spoke again, he hissed through his teeth:

"I'm telling you. Give me my money."

Case was ready, like a rattlesnake about to strike. Jim could see it in his eyes. But surprisingly he seemed to relax for a second. Just for a second. Then his right hand was a blur as it grabbed the short-barreled pistol. But before the gun cleared leather the bore of the Army Colt was against his chest and the hammer was back.

"Wha? Huh?" That was all Case could say, as surprise and shock spread across his broad face. He took a step backward. The bore of the Colt followed him. "Huh?"

Still hissing through his teeth, Jim said, "I told you to do something, mister."

Case's eyes went to his partner at the bar and to the bartender, pleading for help.

Jim growled, "If anybody makes one move, I'll pull this trigger and you'll die. They can't kill me fast enough to keep me from killing you."

In a croaking voice, Case asked, "What . . . whatta you want? I don't know nothin' about no money."

"Yeah, you do. You're the one went through my pockets." With the Colt in his right hand, Jim used his left hand to reach into one of Case's shirt pockets. First one and then the other. Then, eyes still locked onto Case's he reached into a pants pocket and pulled out a roll of bills. Without looking at the roll, he handed it to the bartender.

"I can tell you all about it. It's tied with white string. There are four fifties and two fives. Count it." He didn't take his eyes off Case.

A long moment passed. Then the bartender said, "Why, that's right. That's exactly right."

"Give it to me." The money was placed in Jim's outstretched hand. He stuffed it inside a shirt pocket. "You all saw it. I was locked up in jail for nothing. This gent went through my pockets and stole my money. Let's see if the sheriff will lock him up."

With his left hand, Jim lifted the short-barreled pistol out of the holster on Case's right thigh. "All right, I'm going to get the sheriff. Nobody moves till I'm outside, and then you'd better not point any guns at me. I'll damned sure shoot."

Jim walked backward to the door. There, he holstered the Colt and dropped the short-barreled pistol on the floor. Then he wheeled and walked rapidly down the boardwalk to the sheriff's office. He couldn't walk backward and watch them all the way. He could only hope they wouldn't shoot him in the back on the street. On the way he passed two women carrying parasols to protect their faces from the burning prairie sun. When they were between him and the saloon he let his breath out with a sigh.

Sheriff Rogers wasn't in. Jim sat in the sheriff's desk chair and tried to stop his hands from shaking. That was the closest he'd ever come to shooting a man. It was like Zack Dawson had said, men who got good with guns generally looked for a chance to use them, and sooner or later they'd get the chance. Jim wondered what to do next. And suddenly he realized he'd done something stupid. Something very stupid. He hadn't checked the loads in the Army Colt since he'd dropped it in the creek. If he'd needed it, it might have misfired. Some gunfighter he was.

"Damn, Zack," he said aloud, "if you were here, I'd bend over and pay you to kick me."

He waited an hour for the sheriff. His stomach reminded him it was past noon. He decided to go over to Mrs. Jamison's and give her some money for room and board, then go to the mercantile and give the girl one of his fifty-dollar bills. And while he was in his rented room he'd replace the powder in the Army Colt and put on new primer caps. But he didn't get past Mrs. Jamison.

"I heard about it." She stood in the doorway again. "I don't want no troublemakers in my house."

"You heard about it already?"

"I was just over to the store. A man came in and told ever'body you robbed a man in that saloon. He said you pointed a gun at a man and took his money right there in front of ever'body."

"I only took what he stole from me."

"Well, I don't want no trouble and I don't want no saloon gunmen in my house."

Jim studied his boots a moment, then shook his head sadly. "It's your house. I would like to get my stuff out of the room."

"I'll get it for you. You stay out here."

Meekly, he said, "Yes, ma'am."

With his razor, bar of soap, towel, powder flask, primer caps, and lead bullets wrapped in his blanket roll,

Jim went back to Butler's barn and packed everything inside his saddlebags. Everything except the two blankets and a six-by-six sheet of canvas. Those he rolled up tight. Carrying everything, he went next to the mercantile, wondering if the girl believed what everyone in the store had been told: that he was an armed thief. He wanted her to believe in him. Whether she did or not, he could at least give her her fifty dollars.

But she wasn't there. Woodbine, the store owner, had a hard set to his face when he said, "She went to her house for a late dinner."

"Well" — Jim took the roll of money from his pocket and peeled off a fifty — "if I don't see her, give her this, will you? And tell her thanks again for me."

Woodbine reached for the money cautiously, as if he was afraid it would bite. "Is this some of the money you — "

Jim cut him off. "It's my money." He wheeled and left the store, letting the screen door slam behind him.

Now what? Several days to kill and no place to sleep except on the prairie. Well, he'd slept on the prairie a good many nights. He had to have something to eat, though. Jim hefted the saddlebags and blanket roll across his left shoulder and headed for the clapboard building with an "EATS" sign painted over the door.

Inside, he stopped in the doorway and let his eyes rove over the half-dozen customers. Case wasn't among them. Everyone stopped dead still when he came in, including a man with a spoonful of beans halfway to his mouth. For several seconds, Jim felt like backing out. He was embarrassed at being the center of attention, and he sure as hell didn't want any more trouble. Like the saloon, the cafe held a few tables and a long wooden counter. A half-dozen stools lined the counter. The waiter behind the counter was an old man, bald, with a handlebar mustache and a dirty white apron tied around his middle. Jim's mind told him to leave, but it also told him to stay. He hadn't done anything disgraceful. So he was a stranger. Surely, strangers had stopped here before.

With determination he stepped up to the counter and took a seat. A hand-written menu was tacked to the wall. He decided to order a ham sandwich and a bowl of bean soup. He'd had only a few opportunities to taste ham, and he sure liked it.

But no one came to take his order.

Still embarrassed, Jim looked to the old man with the dirty apron. "Excuse me, sir, but could I have a ham sandwich?"

The old man looked at someone in the kitchen, someone out of sight. Then he looked back at Jim and bobbed his head in the affirmative.

"And a bowl of bean soup."

Another bob of the head.

He could feel eyes on him, but when he turned half-around on the stool everyone quickly looked away. Well, at least they weren't itching for a fight. He wished he'd taken a seat where he could watch the door, in case one of the men from the saloon came in. He should have thought of that before he sat down. That reminded him again that he was no gunfighter.

The soup was delicious and so was the sandwich, but he ate hurriedly, wanting to get outside away from the stares. He paid with one of his five-dollar bills and got his change in silver. It felt heavy in his pocket. Turning to leave, he suddenly recalled something Mrs. Nance had said: "It pays to be nice to folks, as you never know when you'll meet them again." He didn't feel like being nice, but he forced a small nervous smile and said to the waiter, "Mighty fine chuck. Thank you kindly."

The eyes were on him as he stepped through the door and out onto the sidewalk.

Sheriff Rogers still wasn't in his office. Jim was standing in the middle of the room wondering what to do when one of the men he'd seen in the cafe went past. The man had a bushy beard and jackboots. He glanced through the door, stopped two steps beyond it, turned back, put his head inside, and said, "You lookin' for the law?"

"Yeah. Know where he is?"

"Seen 'im a-ridin' outta town headin' east. Said he was a-goin' over to Sand Creek, to the reservation, and wouldn't be back for a day or two."

"Oh. Thanks."

"Them bucks are at it agin."

"Who?"

"Them damn redskins. The gov'munt made a deal with 'em and gives 'em ever'thing and still they steal white men's stock."

Interested, Jim said, "They do?"

"Yeah. Shur'ff's gonna have a medicine talk with them chiefs and see can he put a stop to it."

"I thought the Indians were peaceful now."

"Most of 'em are, but some a them young bucks don't always do what their chiefs tell 'em to."

"Yeah." Jim mulled that over, then allowed, "Well, I reckon there's no use waiting here, then."

"Shore ain't." The bearded one was gone, boots thumping on the plankwalk.

Indians. The word made Jim's blood turn cold. He'd seen them, seen his dad and uncle trade shots with them, seen what they'd done to his mother.

They'd—Forget it. You've got to forget it, he told himself. Just forget it now. He pushed his hat back and dragged a shirtsleeve across his forehead. Push it out of your mind.

Yeah, that was just one of many memories he had to push out of his mind. He'd tried. He was still trying. But it sure was hard to do.

Chapter Thirteen

With at least six hours of daylight left, Jim Waggoner decided to walk east along Apache Creek to the dugout. He hoped the shovel he'd bought was still there. If no one bothered him he could dig up some kind of memento, the picture of his dad and mother, and then when the message came from Pretty Prairie, Texas, he could collect his horse and saddle and be on his way.

On his way where?

He had no plan, except to drift. Go back to Texas or New Mexico or some place where he'd never been. Arizona. California. He'd done some drifting, and he liked seeing strange places. But he knew that one day he'd tire of that kind of life and want to pick a good spot and stay in it. One day.

As he walked, carrying the saddlebags and blanket roll, he recalled the way it had started. They'd put him on a wagon train that came by Apache Creek the next day. "Be a good boy and do like you're told and you'll be all right," someone had said. "These folks will take care of you."

There were ten wagons and ten teams of horses. The wagons carried plows and seed grain as well as food and tents. The people were a religious group from Missouri, all farmers, seeking to build a colony at the foot of the Rocky Mountains. The boy had to work, but he was treated fairly. At first the younger children were curious

66

about him, and the older boys considered him some kind of inferior animal. He never was accepted as one of them, but thinking back, Jim realized it was as much his fault as anyone else's. He was too angry, too bitter. Idle children's chatter was the last thing he cared about. The farmers settled near the new town of Denver where they put their horses to work breaking sod. Seed was planted. They did a lot of praying, and they read the Bible every night. The boy had to do his share of reading, and they insisted that he read out loud. It didn't hurt him, and it sharpened his reading skills.

After fourteen months, the farmers began to give up. The climate was too dry. Crops died for the lack of rain. Some took up prospecting, hoping to strike it rich. Others joined the "Gobacks," and loaded their wagons and headed back east, leaving log cabins and plowed— scarred—land behind. The middle-aged, childless couple Jim had been living with offered to take him back east with them. Jim was twelve by then, and he wanted to see more of the new west. So, with the clothes he was wearing, two dollars cash, a loaf of bread, a slab of cured bacon, and two blankets thrown over his shoulders, he said good-bye and started walking south. They prayed for him and were still praying as he walked out of sight.

Thinking back, Jim shook his head sadly. They were good, hard-working people. Maybe a little fanatical in their religion, but always honest and fair. He'd thought of them often since then, and he hoped they'd found what they were looking for.

He'd walked four days, following a wagon trail along the Front Range, and sleeping under the scattered tall coniferous trees. When a string of mule-drawn freight wagons caught up with him, he hitched a ride. For the next six days he chopped firewood, harnessed and unharnessed mules, led them to water, cut grass for them with a scythe, and washed dishes. He stared in awe at the mountains when they went over the Raton Pass, and he liked the smell of the high country air. At Santa Fe, he got a job cleaning corrals at a livery barn, and was allowed to sleep in the hay loft. The dark-skinned people in their big hats and bright-colored clothes were fascinating, even though he couldn't understand their language. There was always music and laughter in the plaza. Though he was still grim-faced, with a head full of bad memories, Jim enjoyed the music. He would have considered Santa Fe the closest thing to heaven had it not been for the fat Anglo he worked for.

Working hard twelve hours a day was never enough. He was called a bum and was reminded at least twice a day that he would have starved were it not for the generosity of his boss. The money he was paid was barely enough to eat on. At times he had to skip the noon meal. His clothes were ragged and his shoes were nearly worn out. Finally, early one morning he watched men hitch up yokes of oxen, learned that they were returning to Kansas City after hauling twelve wagonloads of trade goods to Santa Fe, and yes, he could go along if he was willing to work.

He worked. The oxen were so slow he could have walked faster, but no one was in a hurry. The traders had made a good profit and were happy to take their time. They couldn't make another trip until next year anyway. Grass for the animals was plentiful and the weather was good. All they had to worry about was the Indians. The damned Comanches.

Men's eyes were constantly scanning the terrain, and men's hands seldom let go of the long-barreled rifles. The boy knew about Indians, the Arapahos and Cheyennes up north, but he didn't tell about what had happened to his mother. He didn't want to talk about it. He didn't want to talk about anything. Twice, Indians were seen at a distance, but there was no attack. At Pretty Prairie, in the Texas panhandle, the boy saw a man on the street wearing a cattleman's clothes, and he politely asked for a job. The man was George Walls. After questioning the boy closely about where he'd come from and who his folks were,

George Walls hired him. And young James Waggoner had found a home on the vast Double O Ranch.

The shovel was still there. Jim climbed to the top of the bluff, stood bareheaded over his mother's grave a moment, then climbed down and resumed digging. He knew he would be helpless in the dugout if anyone came up on him, threw a gun on him. There was nothing he could do about it. He dug.

It was turning dark in the dugout when his shovel struck something hard. It wasn't a bed. He'd already dug the beds out. It had to be the wooden box his mother kept her good china and her good dress in. Digging faster, he uncovered the lid and pried it open with the tip of his shovel. The dress was there, but not the china. Strange. Working fast, he pulled the box aside and dug under it. The tin box he remembered was only a few inches below the dirt floor. With trembling fingers, he opened it. The daguerreotype was there. Also in the box were ten double eagles, each worth twenty dollars.

He carried the picture outside where the light was good and studied his mother's face. The picture was turning brown with age, but he immediately recognized her smile, her blonde hair, and her pert, short nose. His father had a handlebar mustache and a stern look on his face. His brown hair was parted in the middle and slicked back. A penned message under the picture said merely: *Just Married James and Matilda Waggoner San Antonio Texas 1848.*

For a long time he sat on the ground, looking at the picture, but not seeing it. Instead he was seeing his mother, a woman who could find something to be happy about no matter how hard life was. A pretty woman, soft spoken, always kind to animals, well-mannered. A lady in every sense of the word.

This was what he'd come here for. This was worth being shot at and jailed.

And then a dark memory came to his mind, and he felt like blubbering. The way his mother had looked when they'd come home and found her — on the ground, spread-eagled, her dress up over her waist. Her throat cut.

Oh, God.

Damned Indians. God-damned savages. God-damned stinking bloodthirsty sons of bitches.

Jim Waggoner pushed his hat back and dragged a shirtsleeve across his eyes. No use hating them. His mother wouldn't have wanted him to spend the rest of his life hating anyone. Besides, there were white men who were just as bad. Even worse.

The sun had gone down when Jim Waggoner stood. He went back inside the dugout and picked up the tin box. He tried to guess what had happened to his mother's china dishes, and couldn't. They could have been stolen, but a thief would have no use for a set of dishes. Well, whoever took them hadn't dug under the box they were in and found the tin box and the picture. The picture was the important thing.

It was too dark to see inside the dugout now, and Jim groped his way outside, leaving the shovel. He pushed the tin box into one of the saddlebags, hefted them and his blankets over his shoulders, shifted the Army Colt to a more comfortable position, and started the walk back to town.

The range of mountains far to the west made a jagged edge on the horizon, just a shade darker than the sky. Cottonwood leaves rustled in the breeze, and the creek made soft gurgling sounds. It was Jim's favorite time of day, a time when the day's work was done and food and rest awaited. It was a time for pipe-smoking and storytelling. Jim had tried smoking and didn't like it, but he did like listening to the stories older men had to tell.

Except for lamplights in the windows, the town was dark. A light was burning in the cafe, so Jim went there. Again, all activity stopped when he stepped inside, but this time he wasn't so embarrassed. He sat at the counter and put the saddlebags and blanket roll on the floor at his feet. The same old man waited on him, but now he spoke: "Roast beef, smashed spuds, and water gravy. That's it. What'll you have?"

"How about some beef, potatoes, and gravy?"

No one tried to make conversation with him while he ate. There was very little conversation anywhere. He paid with some of the silver he had in his pocket, and left, carrying everything he owned except a horse and saddle.

He considered going to the Prairie Rose saloon and drinking a mug of beer just to kill time, but he didn't want to get into a fight with anyone. Well, there was nothing to do but find a place to spread his blankets and bed down for the night. Tomorrow he'd . . . what? Nothing. Wait.

He'd been to the creek behind Butler's barn twice now, and he had no trouble finding his way there in the dark. He stayed on this side of the creek, under the cutbank, preferring not to get his boots wet wading. By groping with his hands, he found a sandy spot where he dropped his saddlebags and blanket roll and sat. At first it was pleasant, leaning back on his elbows, looking up at the sky. There was a shooting star. Then another one streaked across. Where did they go? What made them go? Were they falling out of the sky somewhere or crossing the sky? If they fell, where did they land? Did anybody ever find one on the ground? Someday, people would know the answers. People were learning more all the time. The smart people. He wished he were one of the smart ones. No, he wouldn't want to spend his time looking through spyglasses and making calculations on paper. He liked the out-of-doors: plenty of room, horses and cattle. But he was glad that some people were smart.

Looking up at the vastness of the sky made him realize how tiny and insignificant he was. It gave him a lonely feeling. He'd talked to very few people since he left west Texas ten days ago. Or was it eleven days? No matter. The girl, Janet Carbaugh, where did she live? Did she live

71

with her family? Lord, he wished he had someone to talk to.

Then he heard men's voices.

Sitting still under the cutbank, he listened. They talked in whispers, but he understood most of what they said. "He's somewhere around here. I seen 'im headin' this way, packin' his stuff."

"Mebbe we oughta wait a while. There's gonna be a half-moon tonight."

They were looking for him, and they had meanness on their minds. Slowly, quietly, Jim lifted the .44 from its holster. He was afraid to thumb the hammer back, knowing it would make an unmistakable sound.

"Prob'ly down on the crik. Be quiet."

He heard them slide down the cutbank. Soon they would stumble over him. Unless he moved. And if he moved he would be heard. Trying to make no sound, Jim put the saddlebags and blanket roll over his left shoulder and stood. Carefully he put one foot in front of the other. It was hopeless. He couldn't walk without being heard. How many men were looking for him? At least two. Maybe more. Two or a dozen, they could throw enough lead around to make things hot and dangerous. Stand perfectly still. Maybe they would go on past him.

No such luck.

"Job and me'll look under the bluff. You two along the water. We'll flush 'im out."

There were four. He could see a dark blob coming his way. It was one of them. Nothing to do now but run. Run and hope. He waited, barely breathing, until the blob was in front of him. He could make out the man's hat and shoulders. Waited. Now.

He swung the gun barrel at the man's head, felt it connect with a sickening thud, saw the man fall. But there was another blob, another man.

"Hey, Case, what happened? Hey, Case is down. That sumbitch is over here."

Run. Jim jumped over the prone man and started running downstream, then changed his mind and went back to the path that led to the top of the cutbank. A shot split the stillness of the night. Two more shots. He could feel heat from the lead balls as they whined past. He was at the path, and he started climbing.

Something hit him in the back, up high, hit him so hard it knocked him down.

Damn. He was shot. No, he could still move. Jim jumped up and started climbing again. More shots. At the top he ran, the saddlebags and blanket roll bouncing on his left shoulder. He ran around Butler's barn and headed toward the town lights. Then he changed his mind and ran west to the railroad tracks. There was nowhere to go. All he could do was try to find a place to hide and wait for daylight. They wouldn't shoot him in sight of the townspeople.

He kept going. Again he was running in the dark, and again he was being shot at.

Chapter Fourteen

The shooting had stopped. Jim could no longer hear men running behind him. They had given up the chase, or hoped that one of their bullets had dropped him and he was lying on the ground in the dark. A train whistle came from the east, far away. He slowed to a walk and tried to figure out what to do. If the chase was over, he could wait it out somewhere on the edge of town. In the morning, townspeople would ask each other what the shooting was all about. Case and his cohorts would think of a way to blame it on him. Yeah, they could say they went to Butler's barn, minding their own business, and the Waggoner boy started popping away at them. They could say they'd caught him trying to get away on the roan horse. In fact, they could be in the Prairie Rose right now, cursing him. The Waggoner boy had come to town carrying a grudge, and was nothing but trouble. Everyone knew that. Apache Wells was a quiet, peaceful town until he came along. The townsmen had to get rid of him before he killed someone.

The train whistled again, closer this time.

The sheriff wouldn't get back for a day or two, and it would still be several days before a message came from Texas. He would have to be mighty careful, not step on anyone's toes, and keep himself better hidden at night.

Standing here on the edge of town wasn't the way he wanted to spend the rest of this night. He turned and walked back toward the creek. The best place to hide was near the creek in the tall weeds and sunflowers. He would be able to hear men coming. Stumbling over tufts of prairie grass, he walked west, expecting to come to the creek a half-mile farther on. The creek meandered here like a snake's track, and as soon as he came to a bend in it, he would try to find a comfortable spot. Stumbling again, he realized he'd stubbed his toes on the railroad. Yeah, the railroad came from the east, caught up with the creek near town, and followed it west a ways. As he remembered from his boyhood, Apache Creek came from somewhere north of Denver and wound its way southeast. He was on the railroad now and a train was coming.

The big engine *whuff-whuffed,* hissed, and blew steam as it pulled into town. Big drive wheels screeched and slid on the rails, bringing everything to a rattling stop. Lanterns bobbed in the night as the crew climbed down from the cab and someone from the one-room depot came out to meet them. A big lantern on the front of the engine put out a little light, but not much.

Jim Waggoner stood in the dark, watching and thinking. He had his money back and he'd found more money in the family dugout. He had time to kill, but killing time in Apache Wells was dangerous. He could get on that train and go to Denver, stay a few days, and come back. By then the sheriff would know he was no horse thief, and he could saddle his roan horse and be on his way somewhere else. Thinking of the double eagles and the tin box he'd found in the dugout, Jim took the saddlebags off his shoulder and opened one to be sure they were still there. And suddenly he knew what had knocked him down back there on the cutbank. A bullet. It had hit the saddlebag that was hanging over his shoulder. Groping with his fingers, he was sure of it. The bullet had torn through the leather, but had flattened and stopped when it hit the tin box and the gold coins.

By rights he should be lying at the bottom of the cutbank with a bullet in his left shoulder.

Well, no time to think about that. He was going to get on the train. Or could he? It wasn't too late to buy a ticket, but they'd see him. Case and his cohorts. They could board the train too, and in Denver he would be an easy target. In a city, people were killed every day, and his murder would look like a simple robbery murder. No, better to get on the train without being seen. If he could.

He stood on the dark prairie and waited.

The big engine *whuff-whuffed* again, spun its drive wheels, and pulled ahead about a hundred yards to the water tank. Lanterns bobbed again as men climbed to the top of the tank. It took some straining and wrestling to get the big spout into the top of the engine's boiler, but once in place it soon filled the boiler. A few minutes after that, the wheels spun some more. Puffing and hissing, the engine jerked the first car, which jerked the next, and on down the line of cars until the whole train was moving.

Jim dropped to the ground until the engine was past, then stood and watched for a chance to grab a ladder on the side of a boxcar. When a car went past in the dark, he ran alongside and found the car empty and the big wide door open. Running, he got his hands on the wooden floor in the doorway, jumped, and got his chest across the doorway. Then, kicking and scrambling, he worked his way inside.

The train was picking up speed, and he knew that if he'd waited another half-minute he wouldn't have been able to run fast enough. As it was, he still had his belongings and he was traveling.

At first he stood in the door and watched the prairie night go past. Tall cottonwoods along the creek were barely visible in the night sky. Then the creek turned north while the train went straight west, and there was nothing to see. Jim sat cross-legged on the boxcar floor, and finally, using his blanket roll for a pillow, he stretched out on the floor. While the boxcar rattled, swayed, and shook, he slept.

Daylight awakened him, a pale morning light. Snorting awake, he sat up and blinked the sleep out of his eyes. He stood, stretched, and realized that the floor of the box-car was dusty, and that he was covered with dust himself. Slapping at his pants legs and shirt, he beat as much of the dirt off himself as he could, shifted the Colt to a normal position, then stepped to the door and looked out. Apache Creek was nowhere in sight. Back they way he'd come there was nothing but rolling prairie. Ahead were a few clapboard shacks. Oh-oh. Quickly, he stepped back out of the door where he couldn't be seen by anyone in the shacks. The train went past them without slowing down. When he looked out again, there was nothing man-made in sight. How far was it to Denver? When he was a kid, folks had guessed it was eighty miles to Denver from where Apache Wells now stood. How fast was the train traveling? Faster than a trotting horse. Maybe about the same speed as a slow gallop. At that speed, they ought to be pulling into Denver soon.

It would be good to find a hotel with hot water and a bathtub. And a restaurant. First thing he'd do was eat, then buy some clean clothes, take a bath, and try to feel human again. Thinking about that, he was glad the train had come along and he was going to a big town.

His stomach was growling when the first buildings came into sight. There were long, low warehouses along the railroad, then a series of buildings with a tall smoke-stack over one of them. Jim wanted to keep out of sight, but he wanted to see ahead too. He took a chance and looked ahead, peering around the edge of the door. The train was slowing. There were more buildings, big build-ings. Then a bridge. An arroyo filled with small trees and tall weeds ran under the bridge. The train was stopping. He had to get out before it came to a standstill. If he didn't, someone would probably walk along the tracks, look inside the boxcar, and see him.

Hefting the saddlebags over his shoulder, he waited until the train slowed to a crawl, then sat in the door with his legs outside, turned so his stomach was on the edge, and slid out backward. He hit the ground on his hands and knees, and skidded on the black gravelly roadbed. His pants were torn, and the skin on his left palm was torn. Standing, he looked around to see what he could see. More buildings were ahead. And there were men near the buildings staring at him. They knew he'd just jumped out of a boxcar.

Jim didn't know whether the men were a threat to him, but he didn't want to take a chance, so he walked back the way he'd come. Glancing over his shoulder, he could see the men watching him. He walked until he came to the bridge with the small trees and weeds below it. He climbed down into the arroyo and pushed his way through the weeds.

And there he saw three more men. Ragged men. As dirty as he was. They stared at him, measuring him with their eyes. One wore bib overalls with suspenders, and another had on baggy wool pants pulled tight in the middle with a piece of rope. They eyed the pistol on his hip and the saddlebags over his shoulder. Finally, the shortest of the three spoke:

"He's not a bull. He just jumped off the westbound, I'll bet."

"Say, boy," said another, "you got anything to eat in those satchels?"

"Eat? Why, uh, no," Jim said, not sure of what to expect from these three.

"What you got there?"

"Why, uh, nothing." He saw no weapons on them.

"The bulls see you with that hogleg they'll throw your ass in the calaboose, and if you shoot one of 'em they'll get the whole U.S. Army after you."

"Well, I reckon I'd better not let them see me."

"You sure you ain't got nothin' to eat? A piece of bread or anything? We ain't et since yestiday mornin'."

"No, I haven't."

"Where'd you come from? How come you're hoppin' freights? Got some kin in Denver? Got any money? If you're plannin' on bummin' somethin' to eat, you'd better shuck that pistol."

"I'm not, uh, I've got enough money to eat on. You're really hungry?" Jim knew what it was like to be in a strange town without a cent and nothing to eat. He unbuttoned a shirt pocket, took out his roll of money, and peeled off the remaining five-dollar bill. "Here, this'll keep you from starving for a while."

The short one took the bill from his hand. "Got any more money?"

The biggest of the three, a man in a billed cap, moved with slow threatening steps toward Jim. Speaking out of the side of his mouth, he said, "You see the size of that roll? He's got a roll of money there big enough to choke a mule. He ought to give us some more of it." To Jim he said, "Hand 'er over, mister, or we'll break both your arms and legs." All three moved closer, menacing.

Backing up a step, Jim said, "I just offered you more than anyone ever gave me."

"You got a lot more. Hand 'er over." The smallest one took a long-bladed knife from somewhere in his clothes. They were all within reach now.

But they stopped suddenly.

The Army Colt had jumped into Jim's hand and was pointed at the knife-wielder. With a curl in his lip, Jim said, "You'd better take what I offered and be glad you've got it. I'm going. Stay away from me."

"Jaysus Jones, didja see 'im draw that gun? Whatever you say, mister."

Jim backed up a few steps, holstered the Colt, then turned and climbed out of the arroyo. He crossed the railroad and kept going until he came to a road. Walking with swift steps, he headed west toward the city of Denver.

Chapter Fifteen

The news was all bad. Some men had caught James Waggoner trying to saddle his horse at Butler's barn and had traded gunshots with him. At first they thought he might be dead or wounded and lying in the weeds along the creek, but after a dozen men had searched the weeds for two miles in each direction, they decided he was in hiding somewhere.

"You're lucky you got your bail money," Mrs. Tuttle said as she placed a sack of flour and a sack of sugar on the long store counter. "But when Sheriff Rogers gets back you'll have to give it up. That young hoodlum stole the money at gunpoint, you know."

Janet didn't know what to believe. "I'm not so sure he's a hoodlum, and I'm not so sure that money isn't his. Those same men shot at him before. You can't take everything they say as the whole truth."

"He came here to shoot somebody because of what happened to his pa and uncle eleven years ago. He came here to get revenge. It's a good thing for him Mr. Tuttle's in Denver or he'd see to it that that young man was disarmed and locked up in jail till he'd be glad to leave town."

"Mr. Tuttle was the judge of the people's court back then, wasn't he?"

"He certainly was. He was the best educated and the most qualified man around here. Why, he'd been to Washington and everyplace."

Janet's dark hair had been combed and brushed until it formed a soft cloud around her oval face. "I was wondering, Mrs. Tuttle, why you and your husband came here. I mean, he was so well-traveled and well-educated, why settle here where he had no chance to use his education?"

"Because the land was free for the taking, that's why. He wanted to go into the cattle business."

"But . . ." Janet's brow wrinkled. "As I understand it, Mr. Tuttle changed his mind and sold his land to Raymond Whitfield."

"Yes. He decided to go into politics instead, but when President Lincoln didn't make him governor, he decided he'd stay here. That's why he built our house in Apache Wells."

Janet finished the story: "Then he was elected to the state council, and now he spends most of his time in Denver."

"Ahem." Janet's employer got her attention and nodded toward another woman customer.

"Oh, please excuse me, Mrs. Olney." She rushed to a middle-aged woman who had placed some canned baking soda and a sack of sugar on the long counter. "I didn't mean to ignore you." Working fast, totaling figures, subtracting change, Janet repeatedly glanced at Mrs. Tuttle, afraid she would leave.

"Oh, Mrs. Tuttle, I would like to ask you about something else, if you would be so kind as to spare a moment."

"Well." The older woman had to ponder that. "All right, but if you're trying to make excuses for that Waggoner boy, you're wasting your time."

Transaction completed, Janet moved back down the counter to Mrs. Tuttle. "I was wondering, did the people's court or land-claim court or whatever it was called have any kind of written bylaws or code or anything?"

"Of course. Mr. Tuttle did everything proper. But you know, don't you, that all the land records were destroyed when our first house burned down."

"Oh." Janet was disappointed.

81

"But I believe Mr. Tuttle got a copy of the criminal code from Mr. Whitfield and it's in his desk at home."

"Just out of curiosity — you know I've studied the history of Colorado Territory — I was wondering if you could find the copy. I would like very much to read it."

"Why, yes, I believe I can. Mr. Tuttle kept papers like that in his desk at home."

"May I read it?"

"Well, I suppose. If you'll come to the house I'll let you read it, but you mustn't take it with you. Mr. Tuttle might want to keep it."

"Of course. I'd just like to read it. I'll come over at noon, will that be all right?"

Janet skipped her noon meal, and hurried east across the bridge to the Tuttle home, a rambling one-story house made of good lumber with a split-shingle roof. Mrs. Tuttle invited her in and offered her a chair in a large drawing room. The room, with its straight-backed wooden furniture and braided rug on the floor, did not look comfortable. It was not a room where people relaxed. Janet guessed that Mrs. Tuttle spent most of her time in the kitchen or in another room furnished for sewing and reading. Mrs. Tuttle had already found the paper that Janet was interested in, and handed it to her. Janet read:

Criminal Code of the Apache Creek Claim Club

Section 1 Any person guilty of willful murder upon conviction thereof shall be hung by the neck until he is dead.

Section 2 Any person guilty of horse stealing or cattle stealing upon conviction thereof shall be hung by the neck until he is dead.

Section 3 Any person shooting or threatening to shoot another, using or threatening to use any deadly weapons except in self defense, shall be fined a sum not less than fifty nor more than five hundred dollars and receive in addition as many stripes on his bare back as a jury of six men may direct, and be banished from the district.

There were two more sections, but Janet didn't read them. Instead, she asked, "Who were the six men on jury, do you remember?"

"Well, I believe there were only four. Mr. Tuttle was concerned about that, but he could only round up four men. This land was very sparsely populated, you know."

"I understand. It would have been difficult to find six men without taking time to search a wide area."

"Yes. Mr. Tuttle talked about that. Our state courts are supposed to have twelve men on the jury, but in some counties, that is next to impossible."

"And as you said just recently, there was no jail to hold suspects in back then, and the trials had to be arranged hastily. And as our teacher, Mr. Bosley, at the preparatory school said, the only real criticism today's jurists have is that there were no appeals."

"That's exactly what Mr. Tuttle says."

"Do you recall who the four were?"

A worry frown wrinkled Mrs. Tuttle's forehead. "Well, there was Raymond Whitfield, Joe Jamison, a Mr. Brumley or Brumby or something like that, and . . . the other I can't recall. Mr. Brumley went back east, I believe."

"I see. Well, thank you very much, Mrs. Tuttle. I have just learned a little more about the history of this territory."

"Did I hear that you want to teach school?"

"I would like to do that. However, I want to further my education first."

"Why don't you ask your stepfather about that trial? Like I said, he was on the jury."

"Maybe I . . . maybe I will."

She didn't have to wait for an opportunity. Ray Whitfield was one of the customers in the Apache Wells Mercantile that afternoon, and when there were no other customers within earshot, he said:

"I heard all about it, about the Waggoner kid giving you fifty dollars he took out of Case's pocket. You aren't going to keep it, are you?"

"No. As soon as the sheriff returns my fifty dollars bail money, I'll return the fifty dollars to James Waggoner."

"That's Case's money."

"Who said so besides Case?"

"Job said. He was there in the Prairie Rose when that kid shoved a gun in Case's face and took the money out of his pocket."

"Where did Case get that much money? How much do you pay him, anyway?"

The rancher's face suddenly flushed, and he mumbled, "Well, he is my foreman. I pay him more than an ordinary cowhand."

Janet suspected she had touched a sore point, and she pressed on. "Do you believe everything he says?"

"Well." There was some hesitancy, and Janet's mind registered it. "Well, sure. He's my foreman. I have to believe him."

"Why does Case and some others want James Waggoner out of town, out of the country?"

"He's a troublemaker."

Shaking her head, she said, "He had no grudge against Case. Case wasn't here eleven years ago, yet it was Case and some of the Prairie Rose bunch who wanted to take him out of the jail and whip him. Did you have anything to do with that? Are you afraid of James Waggoner?"

The rancher's mouth under the thick gray mustache tightened. "I had nothing to do with that, and I ain't afraid of nobody."

"The boys were merely trying to have a little fun, is that it?"

"They thought they could do the town a favor and run him off."

The conversation was interrupted by Woodbine, the store owner. "Janet, we have shelves to stock."

"Oh, I apologize, Mr. Woodbine. I'll get right to it." Out of the corner of her eye, as she unpacked a carton of corn meal, she saw her stepfather leave. And as she worked she wondered whether Ray Whitfield had as much control over his ranch foreman as he should have. And if not, why?

84

Chapter Sixteen

The closer to the heart of Denver Jim got the more traffic he passed. There were heavy freight wagons pulled by four-horse teams, and there were light one-horse buggies. One of the freight wagons *"whoaed"* beside him. The teamster asked if he wanted a ride. Relieved, Jim climbed up on the high seat. "Gonna be a hot one," the teamster allowed. "Just git off the westbound?" He chirruped to the team, and the wagon moved on.

No use denying it. Anyone could tell at a glance that Jim didn't work in one of the warehouses or lumberyards. "Yeah. I caught a free ride."

"Gittin' to be a lot of free riders." The teamster had several days' growth of whiskers, and dark hair under his floppy black hat. "Gittin' to be a lot of men ridin' them freight cars. Where you from?"

"Oh, I got on back at Apache Wells. I would have bought a ticket, but I was west of town and when the train went by I saw a chance to ride free."

"You're lucky. The railroad bulls're gettin' mean. They carry hogleg pistols and billy clubs, and they've been known to split a few skulls."

"I didn't think about that. I don't believe I'll travel that way again."

"You busted?"

85

"Naw. I can pay for a room and some chuck."

"I see you're packin' a pistol your ownself."

"Yeah. I reckon men in the city don't carry guns."

"Some of 'em do. You ever been in the city before?"

"Not for nine years or so. Last time I saw Denver there were about as many tents as houses."

"She's a-growin'. Now that the railroads're here, ever'-body and his dog is comin' to Denver. We got more laws than we can keep track of, and we got officers of the law to make 'em stick."

"It's not against the law to carry a gun, is it?"

"Naw. Not yet. But there's men in the gov'ment that wants to make it agin' the law. The highbrow saloons and restaurants won't let a man in if he's packin' iron."

"Well, as soon as I get a place to stay, I'll leave this pistol behind."

Casting a sideways glance at him, the teamster asked, "You ain't runnin' from the law, are you?"

"No."

"Take some advice. Dirty as you are, I c'n still see you're a better class than most free riders; and if I was you I'd stay outta them saloons. There's men in Denver that'd cut your throat if they thought they could git a nickel out'n your pockets."

"Sounds like good advice."

The wagon rumbled, empty, for five or six miles, then the teamster *"whoaed"* the team again, and said, "I'm turnin' south here. Yonder is Holliday, er, Market Street and beyond that is Larimer. There's hotels and eatin' houses and ever'thing over there. You say you got money?"

"Enough to eat and sleep on a bed for a while."

"Wal, take some advice and don't give it all to the whores and gamblers."

Jim climbed down. "Thanks for the ride."

Boy, how Denver had grown. Instead of log cabins, tar-paper shacks, and tents, there were fine new buildings of board and batten construction, and, yeah, there were some brick buildings too. The streets were dry and dusty, and wagon traffic raised a cloud of dust on Market Street. The ladies in their fine lacy dresses and cute little lacy hats walked on the plank sidewalks, while the men in creased wool pants, finger-length coats, and cravats at their throats stepped off the planks to make room for them.

Jim stayed in the street, gawking up at the three-story brick buildings. One was four stories high. Unbelievable. Carrying the saddlebags and blanket roll over his shoulder, he dodged wagon and buggy traffic, and gawked. As he walked past a small wooden building with a canvas awning over the sidewalk, he smelled food cooking. A sign painted over the door read: SILVER LODE CAFE." Jim went inside.

In here the counter was of polished oak, and the stools had backs on them. The tables were covered with red checkered cloths. Instead of having to look at a menu written on a wall, he was handed a folded sheet of paper with the fare written in a neat hand. And the waiter was a woman, a pretty, smiling young woman, wearing a clean white apron from her throat to her shoes.

There were two other customers at the counter, both in stiff white collars and coats with lapels. Jim knew he was out of place in his dirty, torn clothes, and he wished he hadn't come in.

"Yes, sir?" the waitress said.

"I reckon I'm too late for breakfast." He hoped that would give him an excuse to leave.

"No, sir. We serve breakfast until eleven o'clock, lunch from eleven until four, and dinner from four until eight o'clock."

"Dinner? Oh, I reckon you call supper dinner."

Instead of answering, she looked at him quizzically.

"Well, I see ham and eggs here. That'd be mighty good."

"How would you like your eggs, sir?"

"How? Oh, uh, fried."

"Would you prefer soft fried or hard fried. On one side

or on both sides."

"Uh, make it both sides, but not too hard."

She scribbled something on a little pad of paper, spun around, and left. Shaking his head with a grin, Jim wondered what a cowcamp cook would say if a cowboy asked for eggs, and what he'd do if the cowboy had the gall to tell him how to cook them.

When the young woman came back with a thick china cup of steaming coffee, Jim said, "Thank you, ma'am." He wished he'd gone to a hotel and cleaned up before coming in here, but he needed a meal. And by the time he was ready to leave, he'd had a very good meal in the Silver Lode Cafe. Everything was fine until it came time to pay.

"Oh, sir," she said, when he unfolded a fifty-dollar bill, "we can't break that. You'll have to take that to a bank."

With a wry grin, Jim said, "I should have known. I'll, uh, can you break a double eagle?" He hefted the saddlebags up onto the counter removed the tin box, opened it, and took out a gold coin.

"Why, I—please wait a moment, will you, sir?" She hurried to the kitchen, and Jim guessed she had to ask her boss. When she came back, she said, "Sir, would you wait just a moment while the manager sends someone to the bank. It's just two doors down, and it won't take more than a few minutes." She didn't offer to give him back the double eagle.

"Well, yeah, I reckon that'll be all right. I should have traded for some smaller coins before I came in."

The other two customers were staring at him. He ducked his head and waited. It took ten minutes, but eventually, she came back from the kitchen and counted out nineteen dollars and sixty-five cents in paper money and coins.

His next stop was the Great Northern Hotel on Larimer Street. "Just get to town?" the clerk asked, eyeing the saddlebags and the heavy Colt.

"Yeah. Got dirty traveling. Hope you've got a bathtub and some hot water."

The room was on the second floor. It was clean and neat with a washstand, a pitcher of water, and a washbasin. A small mirror hung on the wall over the stand and another, bigger mirror was attached to a dresser. Near the one window was a clothes tree with wire hangers. The window opened over a narrow alley. Jim could have spit across to the next building. A water closet with a tub was on the first floor, he'd been told.

But first he needed clean clothes, and before he went to the water closet he unbuckled his gunbelt, left it on the dresser, carefully locked the door behind him, then went looking for a haberdashery.

The evening was cool in Denver, and the air, now that the traffic and dust weren't so heavy, smelled of mountains, pine trees, and clear lakes. Someone had said the city was a mile high. Jim felt good in new duck pants, a muslin shirt, clean socks, and underwear. He had a fresh haircut and his boots had been polished in the barber shop. He'd even wiped the dirt off his hat with a washcloth. The Colt .44 was still in his room at the Great Northern, but his saddlebags and all but a few dollars of his money were in the hotel safe. The saloons and liquor emporiums were coming alive. Music poured out open doors. Jim walked slowly, seeing and hearing everything, enjoying himself. A big sign painted on canvas was stretched across the top of a one-story building across the street. It yelled at everyone that Councilman Chester Tuttle was the Republican candidate for Congressional representative.

Chester Tuttle. Yeah, he'd been told that Tuttle spent most of his time in Denver. A councilman. Yeah — they called the upper house of the legislature the state council. Now Chester Tuttle wanted to go back to Washington and represent Colorado Territory before the U.S. Congress. As Jim understood it, a territorial representative had no vote in Congress, and could only buttonhole those who did.

Well, Chester Tuttle ought to be good at it. He'd spent

some time in Washington, and no doubt knew his way around the nation's capital and the Congress.

And while Jim was thinking about Chester Tuttle, he saw him.

At first he wasn't sure. It had been eleven years, and Jim was only ten when he'd seen him last. But, yeah, that round face under thick dark hair over a short plump body. The thick lips. Short legs. The flare for fine clothes. He was dressed in gray pants with a sharp crease down the front, a vest with a gold watch chain draped from one side pocket to another, a dark blue Prince Albert coat and a gray top hat. And he was the right age — about fifty. He was coming out of a hotel-restaurant with big padded double doors and etched glass in the windows, and he had a young woman on his arm.

Some woman.

Her dress was purple velvet, accented with white lace. She wore a matching hat with a long multi colored feather sticking out. Her red hair was carefully waved over her ears and her lips were painted a dark red. She was smiling. She was beautiful.

But who was she? Jim could barely remember Mrs. Tuttle, the woman who had tried to hold him prisoner back then. Mrs. Tuttle's face wouldn't come to Jim's mind, but she was about the same age as her husband. This woman was only a little older than Jim. The Tuttles had no children. Jim remembered that much about them. This could not be Tuttle's daughter.

A buggy with a canopy, pulled by two handsome bay horses, was waiting for them, and Chester Tuttle helped the young woman in, then climbed in to sit beside her on a padded leather seat. Chester Tuttle didn't do the driving. He spoke to a man in black, sitting on a higher seat. The man clucked to the horses, and the buggy went down the street.

Curious, Jim followed, staying on the sidewalks. When the bay team broke into a slow trot, Jim broke into a run. He knew he couldn't keep up with the horses, but he had to try.

Somehow, it seemed important for him to know where Chester Tuttle was going.

Chapter Seventeen

Jim Waggoner was tiring fast. He'd done a lot of running since he'd left west Texas, and running wasn't something a horseman was used to. The buggy traveled over the dirt streets of Denver, turned a corner, went a block, and turned another corner. By then, Jim was so far behind, he didn't see the second turn, and he lost sight of it. Damn.

Walking now, breathing heavily, he went on up the street, but saw nothing moving. A row of frame houses lined the street. A dog barked at him. He went around a corner, walked another block, then turned back toward Larimer. The houses were bigger here, with trees and shrubs planted in the yards. And here he saw the buggy and bay team.

They stood in front of a two-story house with a wide porch, tall heavily draped windows and a front door almost big enough to drive the team through. The house was painted white with dark trim. Lighted lanterns hung on each side of the door and on posts in the yard. As Jim stood in the street and watched, the man in black spoke to the team, and the buggy moved along a gravel drive to the back of the house. Jim guessed there were stables back there.

If this was where Chester Tuttle was living, he was doing very well for himself. A house in Apache Wells and another, bigger house in Denver. That is, if he owned this house. Maybe he only rented a room in it. The young woman could be occupying another room. Yeah, that was it.

Or was it?

For a moment Jim considered walking up onto the wide porch and knocking on the door. It would be interesting to see who answered his knock. What would he say? If Chester Tuttle answered his knock, would he recognize Jim? Naw. Not right away. What would he do if Jim introduced himself? It would be interesting.

But not tonight. Strangers didn't knock on the doors of private residences at night. He'd come back tomorrow.

The streets in the residential section of Denver were dark, and dogs set up a racket as he walked back to Larimer Street. The lamps on the corners of downtown Denver were a welcome sight, and so were the lamps in front of the saloons and hotels. Jim paused at the hotel-restaurant that Chester Tuttle and the young woman had come out of. It was the finest building he'd ever seen. Brick, but with white wood framing the big etched glass windows. Expensively dressed men and ladies came out and entered buggies drawn by high-stepping horses. The place smelled of money. Walking on down the street, Jim passed a saloon with a wide-open door. He could see bright lights inside and hear a ricky-tick piano. He stopped to listen. The men who came and went wore workingmen's clothes, and they didn't give Jim a second glance. Two men in denim overalls staggered out, holding each other up. They staggered down the street toward the fine hotel-restaurant, then switched directions and came back. As they went by, Jim heard one of them say, ". . . nothin' to do with them swells. Le's go down to the Tollhouse. They got real whiskey there."

Inside, the saloon was crowded with laboring-class men and a few overpainted ladies in brightly-colored gowns cut low at the top and high at the bottom. The piano was near the door, and the pianist was working hard. Jim edged his way up to the long bar, put one foot on the brass rail, and waited for service.

Two bartenders with handlebar mustaches and garters on their sleeves were working as fast as they could, drawing beer out of kegs mounted behind the bar and pouring whiskey out of bottles. Finally, one of them stepped up. "Yeah?"

"Beer," Jim said. It was drawn and placed on the bar before him in a glass mug. "Fifteen cents," the bartender said. It was a nickel more than a mug of beer in west Texas, but Jim paid without a word. Saloons in west Texas had no music.

Turning his back to the bar, the beer mug in his hand, Jim watched the pianist and listened to his music. Lordy, that man had nimble fingers. How could he move his hands and fingers so fast without hitting the wrong keys? Must have taken many years of practice.

But the pianist's hands were no swifter than those of a gambler, a bilk, who was trying to coax men into playing three-card monte. "Here you are, gentlemen," he shrilled, shuffling three cards. "The ace of diamonds is the winning card."

A few curious men gathered around his small table and watched his nimble fingers lay the three cards face-down. "It is my regular trade, gentlemen, to move my hands quicker than your eyes."

A middle-aged man in miner's clothes plunked down a silver coin and picked a card, the wrong card. The bilk quickly pocketed the coin, shuffled the cards again, and laid them out again. "Here you are, gentlemen . . ."

"Hey, cowboy, where you from?" She was young and would have been pretty with less paint on her face.

"Why, uh, not far away."

"I can tell you're a cowboy. Did you drive a herd of cattle to the stockyards?" The perfume she wore was powerful stuff.

"Well, no, uh, I'm just looking."

"Want some company?"

"Well, uh . . ." He didn't much want her company, and

94

he didn't want to insult her. Her perfume would have smelled good if there had been less of it.

"Lots of cowboys come in here. Ever since the railroads built them pens, cowboys've been drivin' cattle here from ever' where."

Glancing around the room, Jim didn't see anyone who looked like a cattleman. Oh, there were men in big hats and boots, but somehow they didn't wear their clothes the way cattlemen did.

"You don't talk much, do you? Like to buy me a drink? We could set over there at one a them tables and have a good visit."

"Well, uh, I, uh, I have to go." Jim drained his beer mug, put it on the bar, turned on his heels, and walked out. As he went through the door, he heard her yell in a shrill voice, "Well, screw you too, mister."

Maybe he'd made a mistake. She wasn't bad-looking, and she was pure female. He hadn't been on a bed with a woman for almost a year. It would have been good, and he could afford it. But when he thought about it, a face came to his mind, an oval face with kind brown eyes, framed with soft dark hair. The pretty face of a girl who cared about people, who, for some reason he didn't understand, cared about him.

Jim realized then that he wanted to go back to Apache Wells. He definitely would go back. He wanted to see her again.

On his way to the Great Northern Hotel, he passed a pile of newspapers with a cigar box on top and a sign that said, *Two Cents*. He dropped a nickel in the box and took a paper. He liked to read, and he hadn't read a newspaper in a long time. With the folded paper in his left hand, he walked into the hotel lobby, nodded at the desk clerk, and climbed the stairs. In his room, he pulled off his boots, sat on the feather-filled mattress and unfolded the *Daily Rocky Mountain News*.

The gray pages with narrow columns and small print were filled mostly with advertisements. A long ad from

L.N. Greenleaf & Co. hawked everything from cigars to musical instruments. Another column advertised the Bull's Head Corral and Stockyard where hay, coal, coal oil, and wagons made by Bishop & Prindle were sold. Still another column was headlined, *Territorial News*. There was a two-paragraph story under it:

The crops around Greeley, wherever irrigation has been properly attended to, look promising . . .

Jim turned the pages until his eyes fell on a headline that said: *Republican Central Committee*. Under that was the message:

In a meeting last evening of the Republican Central Committee, Territorial Councilman Chester Tuttle made it understood that he wants to be the next representative in the U.S. Congress from the Territory of Colorado. Mr. Tuttle asked the committee members to nominate him as the party's candidate. Now completing his second term in the Territorial Council, Mr. Tuttle has been active in politics since the era of the Jefferson Territory. Already known in the nation's capital, Mr. Tuttle was reared in Baltimore, Maryland, and attended Harvard University. As a boy he was a frequent visitor in Washington, D.C. Upon reaching adulthood, he took an interest in politics and spent much of his time as an aide to the elected representatives from Maryland. In that position he became personally acquainted with many members of the U.S. House and Senate.

Like many other young men, he saw the untamed west as an opportunity and a challenge, and was one of the first to settle along Apache Creek. Over the years he acquired large holdings of land and cattle, and was active in trying to establish this area as Jefferson Territory. Failing in that, he went to Washington and was instrumental in persuading the U.S. Congress and President Buchanan to establish the Territory of Colorado. Mr. Tuttle was also instrumental in establishing Denver as the Territory's capital, and in bringing two railroads to the city. It is expected that he will have no opposition in the Republican Party.

Jim Waggoner read the story with interest. So Chester Tuttle was raised in the east and knew his way around the nation's capital. So he had acquired large holdings of land and cattle. Started with a one-room sod shack and a land claim that had no legal status at all, and, over the next eleven years, got rich.

A one-room shack. A lot of men had started that way and grown wealthy. Chester Tuttle wasn't the kind of man who'd be satisfied living a hard life on the frontier. Too ambitious. And smart. Searching his memory, Jim recalled everyone referring to Chester Tuttle as Mr. Tuttle, and speaking of him with a great deal of respect. He was a leader. He was the kind who would get rich if there was any chance at all. He had made his money and gone to Denver where the living was easier. But why had he left his wife behind? And who was that beauty he'd been with tonight?

Jim mulled it over, lay on his back on the bed with his hands under his head, and worried about it. He took off his clothes and crawled between clean white sheets. Before dozing off he decided he would have to learn more about Chester Tuttle's life in the city.

Chapter Eighteen

The man was gaunt, weary looking, slump-shouldered. A gray stubble covered the lower half of his face, and long gray hair hung from under his battered black hat. His overalls were dirty, and the laced shoes on his feet were scuffed and colorless. When he stepped inside the Apache Wells Mercantile, his eyes darted quickly about the large room, then settled on Janet Carbaugh.

"Miss," he said, "we, uh, I just got to town and I'm lookin' for Mr. Tuttle. Chester Tuttle. Can you tell me where I might find 'im?"

"Why, I believe he's in Denver. He serves in the legislature, you know, and he stays in Denver most of the time."

"Oh." The man's shoulders slumped even lower and he seemed to shrink inside the baggy overalls and shapeless shirt. He turned to go, then stopped. "Would you know, ma'am, where a feller could sell a team and wagon?"

Janet could see hopelessness in the man's face, and she wanted to do something for him. "Well, the ranchers around here can always use another team. Sometimes folks with horses to sell post a note on the wall over there."

"We have to take the train to Denver, ma'am, and I need to sell my team and wagon before we go."

"Mr. Butler sometimes trades horses and wagons. I can show you how to find his barn."

"I shore would appreciate it, ma'am."

Janet stepped past him and went out onto the porch. He

followed. "It's over that way, sir, near the creek. It's a big barn. You'll see it as soon as you get around the corner."

She wished she knew somebody who needed his horses and wagon and would pay a fair price. Butler would see the hopelessness in the man's face and offer him next to nothing. She watched him walk down the steps to the street. Then she thought of something that might help.

"Oh, mister, I don't know where in Denver Chester Tuttle lives, but his wife is here in town. Can she be of any help?"

"Maybe." His face seemed to show more life. "Maybe she can. Would you know where I c'n find her, ma'am?"

As she worked, waiting on customers, dusting shelves, sweeping, Janet couldn't get the man out of her mind. It was the weariness and resignation in his face that bothered her. He was a man with serious problems and no solutions. Although, he had shown a spark of optimism when she'd told him where to find Mrs. Tuttle. But why? Then, when Sheriff Rogers strode in, spurs jangling, she had something else to think about.

"Sheriff Rogers, welcome back. Did you . . . ?" She paused, trying to think of which question to ask first.

He answered, "Yes and no. Yes, I met on Sand Creek with a pair of the old chiefs, and they promised to try to make those bucks behave themselves. And no, I didn't get a reply to my message about that roan horse. Maybe it'll come in on the westbound tonight."

"Oh. Well, I hope there'll be no more trouble with Indians."

"Can't promise that. I'm telling everybody to keep their eyes peeled and their guns loaded. And, oh yeah, I heard about that Waggoner boy stickin' a pistol in old Case's face and taking some money out of his pocket. When I see him I'll have to arrest him again."

"That could have been his own money he took, you know."

"It'll be up to the court to decide whose money it is."

"But the judge only comes twice a month."

"That's why I don't ever arrest anybody unless I have to."

"Suppose he gave you the money to hold until the court convenes. Would that keep him out of jail?"

"It might. But I heard he's done quit the contrary. We'll prob'ly never see him again."

"I think we will. While you were hearing everything, did you hear about Case and his cohorts shooting at him night before last?"

"Yeah, I heard he was trying to steal his horse."

"Do you believe that?"

"What else would he be doing at Butler's barn?"

"Well, tell me this, Sheriff: if you get a message from Texas that proves he didn't steal the horse in the first place, would you listen to what he has to say about all the shooting?"

"If that's his horse, then we've mistreated him, and I'll consider anything he's got to say. How's that?"

"Fair enough."

"But that's a mighty big if."

The lawman bought some coffee and pipe tobacco and left. She wished James Waggoner would turn up — but on second thought, maybe it would be better for him to stay hidden until the message came from Texas. If he didn't he'd be back in that gosh-awful jail.

And while she was worrying about that, she saw the tired man in overalls again. Again, he stopped just inside the door and let his eyes settle on her. Woodbine was at the far end of the counter going over his books. The man seemed to step a little livelier now as he came toward her.

"You're Miss Carbaugh, ain't you?"

"Yes, sir, I am. Did you find Mrs. Tuttle?"

"That I did. Her husband wasn't to home, but when I told her what I wanted, she said a feller named James Waggoner was around here somewheres, and she said you might know where I c'n find him."

"I really can't. I wish I could. But I think he's not far away, and I think he'll be back."

"Oh." The hopelessness returned. "Wal, do you know

when he'll be back?"

"Not exactly, but I would guess in a day or two."

"Wal." He looked like a spanked puppy. "Reckon I'll go on over to that barn and see c'n I sell my outfit."

"Sir." She wanted to know what his problem was, but didn't want to ask. "Is it important, what you need to see James Waggoner about?"

"It's important to him. Me too."

"Well, when he comes back, where can he find you?"

"I got to get on up to Denver. My missus is terrible sick and I got to get her up there to a hospital. Our team and wagon is all we got and I got to get enough money for 'em to buy some train tickets and pay a doctor."

"Oh, my. The westbound won't go through here until tonight. Where is your wife now?"

"She's in the wagon out by the crik. She's terrible sick."

"Is she comfortable? Can I do anything for her?"

"I don't know. She ain't laid on a bed for four days now. We come up here from Frenchman's Crik, down south. We got to get on the train to Denver, but we ain't got no money."

"Well, I have a cabin and a bed. If you want to, you can take her there, where she'll be comfortable while you wait for the train."

"Wal, that'd be mighty nice of you, ma'am, Miss Carbaugh. The missus'll shore appreciate that."

"Go and get her. I'll show you where my cabin is and I'll meet you there."

"I'll do that, ma'am. Yes, ma'am, I'll do that right now."

Janet looked down the counter at her employer. "Mr. Woodbine, can I . . . ?" The merchant nodded. "Go ahead, Janet."

"I'll be back as soon as I can."

"Janet." Woodbine was smiling a lopsided smile. "If the world gets any heavier, you won't be able to carry it."

The woman *was* sick. Her lips were dry and cracked and her eyes were only half-open. Janet put a hand on her forehead, and found it too warm. She was barely able to walk, and could only mumble her gratitude at being allowed to

101

lie on a soft bed. Janet recognized the symptoms. Diphtheria, the same illness that had taken her mother. At least, that's what some folks believed it had been. No one knew for sure.

After making her as comfortable as she could, with a cool damp cloth over her forehead, Janet motioned the man outside. "I wish we had a doctor here. The only kind of medicine we have at the store is some Parson's Purgative Pills and some Hostetter's Stomach Bitters, but I'm not sure that would help her."

"Ain't got no money nohow."

"I'd get it for her anyway, but it might do more harm than good. She needs a doctor. If you can't sell your horses, I'll, uh, I'll lend you the train fare."

"That'd be mighty good of you."

"You stay here as long as you want. I've got to get back to the store. Oh," Janet said as an afterthought, "you said you need to see James Waggoner about something important. Where in Denver can he find you?"

"I don't know. At the hospital, I reckon."

"If it's terribly important, maybe you . . . no, you have to get your wife to a hospital as soon as possible. I'll tell Mr. Waggoner what you said."

"It's about the trial."

"What? The trial?"

"Yes, ma'am. The one where they hung his pappy. Back in eighteen hundred and sixty."

"You know something about that?"

"Yes, ma'am. I was there. I was the, uh—what was it Mr. Tuttle called me?—a, uh, plaintiff. Yeah, that was it. And the witness."

"You were a witness?"

"Yes, ma'am. Them bullocks that was stole, they was mine."

"Oh, my gosh. You testified that the Waggoner brothers stole some bulls from you?"

"Oh, no. No, ma'am. I didn't say that. Alls I said is two men run off my stock, and them two bulls was mine. And them bulls was fresh-branded and they was branded with the Waggoner brother's brand. That's all I said."

"Oh, my gosh. But you identified the Waggoner brothers as the men who ran off your livestock?"

"No, ma'am. I said it could've been them."

"Oh, my gosh." Janet absorbed that. Then, "So why do you want to see Mr. Tuttle and James Waggoner?"

The man looked down at his scuffed shoes, glanced back at the cabin door, then looked down again. "Wal, I . . . you been nice to me, and I c'n tell you're a friend of the Waggoner boy, so I'll tell you . . . I know somethin' about that trial that Mr. Tuttle wouldn't want me to tell, and I know somethin' that the Waggoner boy would like to know."

"What? What is it?"

His eyes narrowed at her for a second, then he looked down again. "I need some money awful bad. My team and wagon're worth somethin', but not enough. I got to get my missus in a hospital and pay a doctor and buy some medicine and all that." He looked at her, pleading with his eyes. "I need some money awful bad."

Janet's voice turned cold. "And you want to sell information, is that it?"

"I'm shore sorry, ma'am. You been mighty good to my missus. I wouldn't a done it if I didn't need the money so bad."

"Oh-h-h," Janet groaned as the implications of what she'd just heard went through her mind. "Oh-h-h, my gosh. Well . . . what—where can James Waggoner find you when he gets back?"

"If I c'n sell my outfit, I'll be in Denver in the mornin'. I'll be waitin' in a hospital. If there's more'n one I don't know which one we'll be in."

"Well, all right, all right, I'll tell him. By the way, what's your name?"

"It's Pretts, Miss. Lowell Pretts."

Chapter Nineteen

The Silver Lode Cafe was crowded this early in the morning. All kinds of men lined the counter and sat at the checker-clothed tables. There were men in stiff white collars and cravats sitting alongside men in baggy wool pants and shirts with open collars. Two women in clean white aprons were carrying dishes back and forth between the dining room and the kitchen as fast as they could walk. Maybe, James Waggoner thought, he should come back later. After all, he didn't have to be anyplace at a certain time, and these men had to get to work.

His night on the hotel bed hadn't been as comfortable as he'd expected it to be. Too soft. A man used to sleeping on the ground or on a wooden bunk didn't feel right on a featherbed.

Somewhere a steam whistle summoned men to work in a factory. Another whistle sounded over east. Jim recognized the railroad engine's whistle, and wondered if it was going east or west. He ought to be on it. The sheriff of Apache County should be back and he should have gotten an answer from Texas by now. But Jim didn't want to leave Denver just yet.

All right, he'd wait for breakfast. He was used to it. Most of his life he'd had work to do before breakfast. Wrangle in the remuda. Feed livestock. Milk cows to get milk for the kitchen and to feed dogied calves. Chop firewood. He started walking in the direction that Chester Tuttle's buggy had gone the night before.

Traffic on the streets of Denver was picking up. Each time he crossed a street he had to stop, look, and wait for a wagon or buggy to go past. A man could get run over on the streets of Denver. He had no trouble finding the house. With its wide porch, tall windows, and big door, it was easy to recognize. Now what? Stand outside and holler, "Hello," or hammer on the door or what. Well, he hadn't walked over here just to stand in the street and stare at the house.

Warily, afraid a dog might run out from somewhere and bark at him, or someone show up with a gun and demand to know who he was and what he wanted, Jim walked into the yard, paused a moment to gather his courage, and stepped up onto the porch. After a look around, he knocked, using a brass door knocker on the big hand-carved door.

Nothing happened. A full minute passed before he knocked again. Another minute, and then the door opened a crack and a woman peeked out. It was the beautiful redhead.

"Yes?"

Jim removed his hat, "Excuse me, ma'am, but I'm looking for Mr. Tuttle."

Still peeking around the edge of the door, the woman clutched a pink robe around her throat and said, "Mr. Tuttle is not at home."

"Oh. Well, I apologize for bothering you, ma'am, but could you tell me where I might find him?"

"He breakfasts at the Claims Club and goes to his office."

"I . . . I'm a stranger here, ma'am. Would you tell me where his office is?"

"It's next door to the State Capitol. His name is on a sign out front. You can't miss it."

"Thank you. If you don't mind my asking, are you a kin of Mr. Tuttle?"

"I'm his wife."

Dumbfounded, Jim stuttered, "But I, uh, there's a . . ." He was silent a moment, not knowing what to say next. Then he decided to lie a little. "The last time I saw Mr.

Tuttle I didn't think he had a wife."

"We were married just last month."

"Oh. Well, thank you, Mrs. Tuttle. I'll go to his office."

"If you'll leave your name, I'll tell him you were here."

Jim didn't want to tell her his name, but he didn't know how to avoid it. "It's Waggoner. James Waggoner. I think he'll remember me."

"Very well, in case you don't find him at his office I'll tell him."

"Thank you, ma'am."

For a long moment after the door closed Jim stood on the porch and tried to understand. When it finally soaked in, he went back to the street knowing something about Chester Tuttle that apparently no one else knew. Or — that no one was supposed to know.

Chester Tuttle was living a double life. He was living a lie.

And there was something else: Chester Tuttle was not an honest, honorable, straightforward kind of man.

Janet helped Lowell Pretts walk his sick wife to the railroad depot. The poor woman could barely walk, so Janet held up one side of her while her husband supported the other side. Between them, she managed to shuffle her feet and make it the three blocks to the railroad.

The westbound should be along within the hour, they were told. Thank heavens for the railroad. Mrs. Pretts couldn't survive the trip in a wagon. In fact, Janet worried that she wouldn't make it on a train either. But, she reminded herself, her mother had clung to life for a week after her husband and friends could only shake their heads and prepare for the closest thing to a Christian burial as could be had. Hopefully, Mrs. Pretts could hang on too. A doctor and a hospital could probably save her. A railroad could probably have helped save Janet's mother.

Lowell Pretts had sold his horses and wagon, and as expected he had not gotten a fair price. Butler had taken advantage of him. "I got enough to get her in a hospital in Denver," Pretts said, "but that's about all. I hope they'll let her stay till she's well." He carried two heavy quilts, a pillow, and a tin suitcase. That was all he had salvaged from their wagon.

"Oh, they surely will," Janet said.

"I wish I had some more money. Did you say James Waggoner had some money?"

"I don't know. He had a little. I don't know how much he has left."

"Wal, mebbe Mr. Tuttle can spare some. He owes me."

They sat on a wooden bench inside the depot, waiting. Two other passengers sat across the small room on another bench. Janet was becoming disgusted with Lowell Pretts, but she had to give him credit for doing everything he could for his wife.

"Why does Mr. Tuttle owe you?"

"I can't tell. Not now. Not till I get my missus in a hospital."

"Did Mr. Tuttle put words in your mouth at the trial eleven years ago?"

"I can't tell yet. If that Waggoner gent's got any money, I'll tell him."

"Do you think you can get money from both James Waggoner and Mr. Tuttle?"

"Naw. Not both. Whichever one hands me some money first."

"Mr. Pretts, if you know something about the trial that James Waggoner ought to know, you're being terribly unfair if you don't tell him."

"Mebbe I will. But I need some money bad."

While Janet was trying to think of something to say next, they heard the train whistle. The other two passengers stood and walked outside to watch the train arrive. "She's a-comin'," someone said. They waited until the engine had screeched and hissed to a stop, then helped the sick woman up. "She's sick," Pretts said to the conductor, a man in a black coat and a round black cap with a bill on the

107

front. "I'll help her," the conductor said. Janet stood back and watched the two men half-carry Mrs. Pretts up the iron steps and into a passenger car. The two quilts and the pillow would help make her comfortable on the ride to Denver. Faces of other passengers were pressed against the car's windows from the inside, gawking at what they could see of the town, gawking at the new passengers.

While she walked back to her rented cabin, Janet ran the latest development through her mind. Something had happened at the trial eleven years ago that James Waggoner would pay to learn about, that Chester Tuttle would pay to learn about — no, that Chester Tuttle would pay to keep quiet. And after she'd blown out the lamp and crawled into bed, Janet couldn't sleep. Something was wrong with the trial. What?

Lowell Pretts had been the star witness. He'd seen two men run off some of his cattle. When he found two head of the cattle, they'd been branded by the Waggoner brothers. Yes, that would be evidence enough. Men had been hung for lesser crimes. When she'd asked local citizens about the trial and the hanging, they all were convinced that the Waggoners were guilty. The only thing most folks regretted was leaving the boy homeless.

But Lowell Pretts knew something that most folks didn't know.

Janet would like to talk to James Waggoner about it. When was he coming back? Or — could she be wrong about him? Was it possible that he couldn't hold up under all that had happened to him since he had come to Apache Wells? He'd spent two nights in a suffocating jail, and he'd been chased and shot at twice. Had he started running and just kept on going?

God, she hoped not. She had something to tell him. Something that could be very important. The important thing was that the star witness at James Waggoner's father's trial — Mr. Lowell Pretts — was not an honorable man.

Chapter Twenty

If Jim Waggoner had been comfortable and sleeping well, he wouldn't have heard the soft knocking on his hotel-room door. He sat up. The one window was pitch-black. He wondered who was knocking, and he wondered what time of night it was. Walking on bare feet, he went to the door and listened. The knocking came again.

"Who's there?"

"The hotel clerk," a muffled voice said. "I need to talk to you."

"Now?"

"Yes sir, Mr. Waggoner. Something has come up. Something important."

"Well, wait a minute." He struck a match and lit the lamp, then pulled on his pants and shirt. What the hell did the hotel clerk want this time of night? Couldn't it wait until morning?

Uh-oh. Jim had heard about the footpads in the city, men who would sneak up in the dark and club and stab just to see what they could get out of their victims' pockets. He took the .44 out of its holster where it lay on the dresser and thumbed the hammer back. He hoped whoever was on the other side of the door wouldn't hear the gun being cocked. Still barefoot, he tiptoed to the door and listened. Not a sound came from the other side. Jim stood beside the doorjamb, reached out with his left hand, and slowly slid the latch back. Stopped. Listened.

Still no sound. He turned the knob and opened the door a crack. Listened. Dim lamplight came from the hall. With his left foot, Jim pushed the door farther open, then looked around the doorjamb. Nobody was there.

What the hell was going on here? "Hey," he whispered. "Hey, where are you?"

No answer.

Now what? Shut the door and forget it? Yeah, somebody's playing tricks. Just shut the door, make sure it's latched, and go back to bed. Wonder who was out there?

Later, when he thought about it, Jim knew he'd done something stupid. Curiosity killed the cat, he'd heard. It almost killed him.

Thinking he'd look up and down the hall, he put his head through the door. A sharp pain flashed through his brain, and he felt himself falling. Barely conscious, he hit the hall floor on his face, and felt another sharp pain in his left side. He was losing consciousness now, letting the blackness surround him. He couldn't black out. He couldn't allow it. Something was wrong here. He was in danger. He was about to be killed.

No. Not like this.

His mind told him to roll, and he flipped over onto his back. A dark shape bent over him. A knife blade flashed. The Army Colt roared. Roared again. The dark shape disappeared.

Blackness took over.

He was back on the Double O. He booted the bay colt into a lope to head off a cow that was trying to go back to where she had last seen her calf. Suddenly, the colt's head disappeared and the cantleboard hit him in the seat of the pants so hard he felt it clear up to his neck. Desperately, he grabbed for everything that stuck out on the saddle, trying to keep his seat. The colt squealed like a pig and bucked like a scalded ape. The boy grabbed hold of the coiled rope, and the rope strap broke. He grabbed the saddle horn and pulled the leather cap loose from it. There were tacks under the leather cap, and he cut his fingers on the tacks. His right stirrup flew up and banged him on the knee. He was going down, and the ground was rocky.

"Mr. Waggoner? Mr. Waggoner? Can you hear me? I've already sent for the night marshall. Can you hear me, Mr. Waggoner?"

The lights moved around. The faces above him moved. They appeared and disappeared. His head was a drum and somebody was beating on it. He blinked and tried to focus his eyes. The faces shifted, then steadied. "Huh?"

"The night marshall is on his way, Mr. Waggoner. Can you hear me?"

"Y-yeah." He tried to sit up, feeling the same way he'd felt back in Butler's barn at Apache Wells. Damned if this wasn't getting old. "Yeah, I reckon I'm still alive. What happened? Did somebody try to kill me?"

"We're very sorry about this, Mr. Waggoner. Generally, we don't let things like this happen."

Sitting up now, Jim got his eyes to focus. There were a half-dozen faces around him. Men's faces. He looked at himself. There was blood on his shirt, on the left side. His left side hurt. His head hurt. "Whoo," he said. Then he saw the dead man.

"Oh-h-h. Did I . . . ?"

"Yes sir, Mr. Waggoner. We heard your pistol shots. That man is dead, shot through the heart."

"Oh-h-h boy."

"But don't worry. It was obviously an attempt to rob you. You were clubbed over the head and cut. You fired in self-defense."

"Oh-h-h boy."

Heavy boots clomped up the stairs and came toward him. Men stepped back. "What's goin' on here? Did somebody shoot somebody?"

111

"Yes sir, marshall. Mr. Waggoner is one of our guests and this man here tried to rob him."

Another face was before him, a lean face with a handlebar mustache. "You hurt?"

"I, uh, I'm alive." By holding onto a wall, Jim managed to get to his feet. He was still clutching the .44. Now he could smell the gunsmoke. "He said he was the hotel clerk, and I opened the door. Oh-h-h boy, how dumb can a feller get?"

"Where're you from, mister?"

"Oh, uh, west Texas by way of Apache Wells."

"You better go see a doctor. How bad is that cut on your side?"

Jim's head was still swimming, but he pulled up his shirttail and tried to see the wound. The marshall's head was in his way. "Cut you, all right. If you can stand, it prob'ly ain't too deep. But we're gonna take you to a hospital."

"I'll lock your room up tight, Mr. Waggoner. No one will get in."

As Jim Waggoner walked out of Receiving Hospital, a cab-for-hire pulled by one horse stopped in front and a man and woman got out. The woman was so weak she could barely walk, and the man looked like he'd been out in the hills without food or sleep for a long time. The cab driver carried a tin suitcase and an armload of quilts and pillows in behind the couple.

At least, Jim thought, he could walk by himself and didn't feel too bad.

The cut in his left side took a dozen stitches to close, and he had a knot on the back of his head. Serves me right, he thought, for being so stupid as to stick my head out the door. Son of a bitch was standing right there against the wall with a club in one hand and a knife in the other, just waiting for me to do that.

In the lobby of the Great Northern Hotel, the night marshall was waiting, smoking a stub of a cigar and reading a newspaper. His handlebar mustache looked like it had been waxed, and he carried a pearl-handled silver-plated revolver in a holster under his left armpit.

"Now that you're able to get around by yourself, I've gotta ask you some questions," he said. Wearily, Jim dropped into a wooden rocking chair beside the marshall. "Like, what'd you have in your room that was worth stealin'?"

"Nothing. Nothing but that old Army sixgun."

"You either got something or that hooligan thought you did. You keepin' anything in the hotel safe?"

"Yeah, I've got some cash in the safe."

"Uh-huh," the marshall snorted. "He must of seen you with it. You show it to anybody?"

"No. Well, yeah, yesterday morning, I had to open a tin box and take out a double eagle to pay for my breakfast. There were a couple of men in the restaurant — the Silver Lode — and they might have seen me do that."

"What did they look like?"

"They were well-dressed, like clerks or something."

"Huh-uh. Wasn't them. The man you killed was a street thug. He never wore good clothes in his life."

"Killed?" Until now, Jim hadn't given any thought to the fact that he'd killed a man. It was something to think about. He didn't like it. The stitches in his side stung. He didn't like it at all.

"Don't worry, you didn't break any laws. A man's got a right to defend hisself. I just got to make out a report, that's all."

"Did he, uh, did he have a family, or anything?"

"Don't know. Don't know his name yet. But I doubt it. His kind hangs around lookin' for somebody to rob." The marshall took the cigar stub out of his mouth, looked at it, stuck it back in. "Naw. He ain't got no family. Don't worry about it. You prob'ly done ever'one a favor by pluggin' him."

"Well, could he have seen me in the restaurant, standing back where I didn't notice him, or maybe he saw me carrying my saddlebags, or . . . ?"

"Don't know. He seen somethin', or thought he did."

Shaking his head sadly, Jim allowed, "I never killed a man before, wish it . . . aw, hell."

"Happens all the time. Happens too damned often." He pronounced the *t* in often. "Keeps the coroner busy. A cattleman like you comes to town and some thug thinks he's got some money and waylays 'im. You are a cattleman, ain't you?"

"Yeah, uh . . ."

"Come to town to see the sights?"

"Well, yeah."

Standing, the marshall dropped his cigar stub in a spittoon. "Well, I'm off shift. S'posed to be off a half an hour ago. You gonna stay in town awhile?"

"I don't know. I've got business in Apache Wells. I might catch the next train east."

"Well, understand one thing: you think livin' is dangerous out there in the hills where there ain't no law, but that's a picnic compared to walkin' around on these streets at night with money in your pockets. Watch yourself."

"Yeah," Jim said. "I know what you mean."

Chapter Twenty-one

It was Sunday and the Apache Wells Mercantile was closed for the day. Janet Carbaugh had an early breakfast and went to Butler's barn. Her gray horse was eating hay in a big feedlot, and was easy to catch. She saddled him with a sidesaddle, then led him to a mounting block to get settled in the saddle. With her right leg over the saddle's hook and her long dress arranged to cover her down to her ankles, she rode out of town.

The sun was above the eastern horizon now. Not a cloud was in the sky. It would be another hot day. Janet crossed the Apache Creek bridge and rode past the Tuttle place, past the hanging tree and on past the old Waggoner dugout. There the creek curved southeast toward the far-away Arkansas River. She crossed the creek at the shallow wagon crossing built by men with shovels and horse-drawn fresnos. Four miles out of town she came to the Bar W ranch buildings.

Before she rode into the ranch yard, she reined up. The two-story frame house had once been white and pretty, but paint was peeling off now. Flowers no longer grew along its outside walls, and the shrubbery was dead or dying. The four small cottonwood trees were still growing, however, where her mother had planted them. One horse stood in a corral, but the gates were open on the other pens. Two wagons — a freight wagon and a hay wagon — were parked near the big shed, and a buggy with a canopy on top was parked

115

inside another, smaller shed.

Janet hadn't been here since early spring.

She rode up to the front yard and slid to the ground. Tying the gray horse to a hitchrail she stepped up onto the porch and paused at the front door. No telling what she'd find inside. Readying herself, Janet pushed open the door and stepped in. My gosh, what a mess. The carpet was littered with dirt, cast-aside boots, shirts, and pants. The velvet sofa was dirty and ragged. So were the stuffed chairs. The stair railing was scarred and the carpet on the steps was torn in places. Pictures on the walls hung crookedly.

While Janet was wrinkling her nose in disgust, a man came in from another room. He was bald with a week's growth of whiskers. He wore no shirt; only the top half of his long-handled underwear covered his chest and shoulders. A meat cleaver was clutched in his right hand.

He said, "Oh, it's you, Miss Whitfield. I thought it might be somebody else."

"Who, Poco? Who did you think I might be?"

"Oh, some of the boys. Ray run 'em outta here the other night, and tole 'em to stay out."

"Is Mr. Whitfield here?"

"No, miss. Him and the boys caught their hosses and loped on south early this mornin'."

"Do you expect him back at noon?"

"No, miss. I fixed 'em some flapjacks and beans to carry with 'em. I don't think they'll be back much afore dark."

"Oh." She stood in the middle of the once-elegant living room and shook her head sadly.

"I c'n put the coffeepot on, Miss Whitfield."

"Oh, no thanks, Poco. Tell me, Poco, has the crew been living here in the house?"

"Some of 'em was till Ray finally got mad and run 'em out."

"What's the matter with the bunkhouse? Does the roof leak or something?"

"Not that I know of, miss."

116

Janet looked down, still shaking her head, "Well, has anyone used my room?"

"Oh, no. Ray tole 'em to stay out of that room, and we all knew he meant it."

A sigh came out of Janet. "It's a mess, isn't it?"

The man didn't answer, but shook his head sadly too.

"Well, when Mr. Whitfield returns, tell him I'd like to see him at his earliest convenience, will you do that, Poco?"

"His earliest convenience," Poco said, as if trying to memorize the words. "Yes, miss. I'll be shore to tell 'im."

"I'm going up to my room and then I'm going to go look at my cattle." She wanted to ask him to shave and put on a clean shirt, but what was the use? She had no authority to order anyone to do anything. Besides, Poco was the kind who didn't take orders very well. He'd drifted up from somewhere south at a time when the Bar W needed a cook. The only name anyone knew him by was Poco. That and the fact that he could cook was all they needed to know. "I'll be back before dark," Janet said, "but I won't be staying."

"You be careful, Miss Whitfield."

She climbed the stairs to her room and was pleasantly surprised to find everything in the room the way she had left it. The lace curtains in the window were soiled and the bedspread needed washing, but nothing had been bothered. Janet opened the steamer trunk at the foot of her bed and uncovered the china dishes. Mrs. Waggoner's dishes. They were all there. Then she changed into a pair of boy's cotton pants and a muslin shirt and went downstairs and outside. Leading the gray horse, she went to the big shed, stripped the sidesaddle off, and cinched on a man's saddle. She mounted the horse this time without a mounting block, and, with a leg on each side, she pointed him north.

Most of her cows and calves were grazing over several hundred acres between two low hills about six miles north of the ranch house. Riding at a walk, counting them, she realized that one calf was missing. That wasn't bad. One calf out of sixty-two. Illness and disease always took some livestock. The grass was brown but plentiful and the cattle

117

were in good shape. Riding on, she found the forty-four long yearlings that she was planning to send to Denver in the fall. They would pay for her schooling in the city for another year. With a cattle grower's practiced eye, she could see that the grass was dry and the country needed rain. But she also knew the buffalo and grama grass was just as nutritious after it had been cured by the summer sun as it was in the spring. This was good cattle country.

Silently, she admired the men who recognized the value of this land and who had managed to claim a large part of it. Men like her stepfather, Chester Tuttle, and, yes, the Waggoner brothers. As far as the Washington politicians were concerned, this was desert wasteland. Crops wouldn't grow any farther west than the twenty-inch-rainfall line, which government surveyors figured ran north and south somewhere in western Kansas. They were right. Planted crops died in the field. That was why the U.S. government sold the land so cheap, and that was how a few cattlemen managed to gain control of hundreds of thousands of acres.

They didn't need to plow the land and plant grass. Nature planted it for them. And they didn't need to own that much land. They bought land near the streams, which gave them control of the water, and that gave them control of more public domain than they could ride across in two days. But the far-sighted ones, the smart ones, believed the years of the free range would eventually come to an end, and they bought all the land they could. Men like her stepfather and Chester Tuttle.

They found a ready market for beef in the fast-growing city of Denver, an easy week-long cattle drive from here. And later the railroad construction crews consumed beef as fast as the railroad builders could buy it. Cattlemen got wealthy, while the sodbusting farmers starved out.

Raymond Whitfield had made enough money raising and selling beef to buy out Chester Tuttle. As Janet understood it, Tuttle was the land baron while Whitfield was the cattleman. For years they'd been partners. Then Tuttle

118

had wanted to spend most of his time in Denver, and Whitfield had bought his land. Now Whitfield owned an estimated seventy-five thousand acres. Owned it outright. And about five thousand cattle, which he grazed on his land and on the public domain.

As she rode her gray horse back to the Bar W ranch headquarters, Janet ran it all through her mind. Her stepfather was a cattleman. He knew grass and cattle. Nothing more. Chester Tuttle was the brains behind the partnership. Tuttle had spent a lot of time in Washington. He knew more about the U.S. government and the people in it than anyone else in this territory. What the congressmen were considering and what they were not considering was no doubt filed in his mind. And, Janet surmised, Chester Tuttle was always thinking, trying to find a way to cash in on it.

At the ranch headquarters, Janet didn't change clothes or saddles. Instead she rode up to the back door — the kitchen door — of the main house and yelled for Poco. When he opened the door and looked out, she reminded him to tell Mr. Whitfield that she wanted to see him.

"Yes, miss," Poco said, scratching his belly. "At his earliest convenience. Ain't that right?"

"Thank you, Poco."

On her way back to town, she rode past the Waggoner dugout and shook her head with sorrow. If the Waggoner brothers had lived, they too would be wealthy cattle barons. They'd picked a good spot to settle on. They'd known what they were doing. And then it occurred to her that they had settled on a spot that was right in the way of any expansion plans her stepfather and Chester Tuttle might have had. Did that have anything to do with anything?

She hoped not. But there was certainly that possibility.

Chapter Twenty-two

His head throbbed and the stitches in his side stung, but James Waggoner was glad to be sitting on a seat in a passenger car instead of on the dusty floor of a freight car. The eastbound would pull into Apache Wells about midafternoon, he'd been told. He didn't know what he'd find there. Going back so soon might be a mistake. He had to go back. Not just to gather his roan horse and saddle. That was important. But what was more important was an ugly, nagging suspicion that was building in his mind. It was telling him that the trial and hanging eleven years ago had not been what they were supposed to be.

What made him suspicious was everything that had happened since he'd come back to Apache Creek. He was locked up in jail for a crime he didn't commit, he was shot at in the dark twice, and he was nearly clubbed and stabbed to death in a Denver hotel.

The big questions were: Was it a scheme? Whose scheme? Why? And how to find out?

The passenger car swayed and rattled on the rails as Jim tried to understand it all. An elderly woman sitting next to him on the wooden seat was thrown against him. She begged his pardon, straightened herself, and resumed looking out the window. "It's all right, ma'am," Jim said, trying not to be thrown against her.

He'd killed a man. That was something he'd hoped he'd never have to do, and he didn't like it. But the man had tried to kill him. Damn near did. The old Army Colt had saved his life.

And while he was sitting there, looking out the window without seeing anything, trying to sit still, Jim got to thinking about the man who'd sold him the gun. Zack Dawson.

Jim had spent most of a winter with Zack in a New Mexico line camp. That was after he'd gotten the wanderlust and had drifted away from the Double O to see what the rest of the country looked like. He'd drifted all the way to Arizona, worked in a silver mine there, then drifted back east to Santa Fe, hoping to find the town as lively and musical as it had been years earlier. He wasn't disappointed. There were still guitars, castinets, and gaiety in the plaza. He liked Santa Fe. But he didn't like working in barns and warehouses, and he got homesick for the wide-open country and horses. When he got a chance to hire on with a big New Mexico cow outfit, he did. At first he camped with a crew of cowboys and a chuck wagon, then was assigned to winter in a one-room line shack with Zack Dawson.

Zack had been an Indian fighter, an Army scout, a cattle and horse trader, and a deputy marshal. He knew guns and gunfighting. He was also a philosopher who liked to talk. Jim was the opposite. He volunteered very little about himself. But after sharing a cabin with Zack for a month, he eventually told about his boyhood and what had happened on Apache Creek.

Except for the praying and Bible-thumping, Zack gave him pretty much the same advice Mrs. Nance had given him. Jim remembered it well.

"Son," Zack had said as he chewed a cheek full of cut plug, "you can do one of two things." He spat a stream of juice onto the ground near where they were sitting in an empty cattle pen. "You c'n go back up there to Colarady or whatever name they're gonna give that country and fire that there hogleg at ever'body that had anything to do with it, or . . ." Another splat ". . . you c'n put it out of your mind and grin and laugh and dance with the ladies and drink a little whiskey now and then and stay alive.

"Now"—splat—"you have to figger in the percentages. Figger it this way: if you go back up there and kill somebody, you'll get hung your ownself. Or you'll be on the run and you'll be hunted by the law for the rest of your life."

Splat. "Me? I seen Injuns kill some a my best friends and I seen the carcasses of my friends with the ha'ar cut off and their peckers and balls cut off, and I got ever' right to hate the bloodthirsty sons of bitches." Splat. "And I got to admit that ever' time I see an Injun, no matter how much he grins and pertends to be friendly, I feel the ha'ar on the back of my neck a-risin' and I have a turrible itch to haul out my old forty-some-odd and blast away."

Splat. "But you know what? I'm sixty-five years old—maybe sixty-six—and I'm not done livin'. I still like a drink of whiskey and I like to play a good game of cards and I like to dance with the ladies, and I ain't a-goin' to throw my life away over some worthless blanket-ass Injun."

Splat.

Eventually, Jim had drifted back to the Double O, but instead of staying in the cowcamp with the Nances, he was sent instead to the headquarters near Pretty Prairie to break colts. He thought a lot about what Mrs. Nance and Zack had said, and he vowed that when he was twenty-one he'd go back to Apache Creek. But not for revenge.

Now?

The train's shrill steam whistle brought him out of

his memories, and signaled that they were coming to Apache Wells. Jim kept his seat until the train stopped, afraid he'd fall if he tried to stand. Then, when the conductor got out and placed an iron footstool on the ground, he climbed out too. He was the only passenger to get out at Apache Wells, and the stationmaster stared at him as if he'd seen a ghost. Jim was recognized.

To hell with him. To hell with all of them. Except the girl at the mercantile, Janet Carbaugh. He wanted to see her, but he could think of no excuse for going to the mercantile. Carrying his saddlebags and blanket roll, Jim walked to the sheriff's office. Empty. Wouldn't you know it. Well, hell.

Then he saw the sheriff coming, walking up the sidewalk. He waited.

"Heard you got off the eastbound, young feller. Figured you'd be wanting to see me."

"Yeah."

"Well, I got good news. A Mr. George Walls sent an answer to my telegram. Here, wanta see it?" Sheriff Rogers took a folded sheet of paper out of a shirt pocket, unfolded it and handed it to Jim. It said:

SHERIFF THOMAS J. ROGERS, APACHE WELLS, TERRITORY OF COLORADO. REFERENCE YOUR WIFE. ON MAY 6, 1871, I, GEORGE WALLS, MANAGER OF THE DOUBLE O LAND AND CATTLE CO., TRADED IN LIEU OF WAGES A RED ROAN GELDING FIVE YEARS OLD BRANDED WITH A DOUBLE O ON THE LEFT SHOULDER TO JAMES WAGGONER.

Jim Waggoner read the message twice, then looked at the sheriff. "You can't ask for more than this."

"No. Sure can't. We owe you an apology. I hope you ain't fighting mad about it."

"I sure as hell ain't happy, but I'm not ready to shoot anybody. Not yet. But it seems like nothing ever happens around here without the whole town hearing about it. Did you hear about a bunch of knotheads shooting at me down by the creek? Not just once, but twice?"

"I heard about it. The first time they said you busted out of jail, and the second time they said you was trying to steal your horse."

"I got out of jail, all right, but I didn't try to take a horse. That's a damned lie."

Sheriff Rogers rubbed his jaw and looked down. Two women wearing poke bonnets walked past and stared at Jim. "All right," the sheriff said finally, "you can sign a complaint if you want, and when the judge comes to town I'll see they get to court."

"Who are they?"

"I wish I didn't have to tell you, but you can't sign a complaint unless you know. It was Case, the Bar W foreman, and some of the gents that hang around the Prairie Rose."

"The Bar W belongs to Ray Whitfield?"

"Yeah. Listen, young feller, if you're thinking about taking the law in your own hands, don't do it. Being your own judge and jury and shooting a man is the same as cold-blooded murder."

"What if I'd shot back and hit one of them down at the creek?"

"That'd be different. A man's got a right to defend himself."

"Well, if I shoot somebody it'll be self defense. But I'll tell you one thing, the next time somebody shoots at me I'll damn sure shoot back."

"Know what I want you to do, young feller, I want you to get on your horse and leave these parts. You're trouble looking for a place to happen. Don't make it this place."

"You're not the only one who wants me to leave. Somebody else wants me out of the country or dead, and I want to know why. I'm not leaving yet."

"I could lock you up again, you know, for robbing a

124

man at gunpoint."

"You know why I did that."

"Yeah, but if Case wants to sign a complaint I'll have to arrest you."

"If he signs a complaint against me I'll sign a complaint against him for shooting at me. Will you arrest him?"

"Naw. Can't. You two would kill each other if you were locked up together. Naw, that's why I ain't arresting you."

"Then, I'm going on about my business." Jim turned on his heels and stomped away toward Butler's barn. The sheriff had no more to say.

He had to pay Butler for the horse's keep. "The shur'ff said it's all right to take 'im," Butler said. Jim said no more than he had to. "Expect you'll be driftin' on now," Butler said. "Not yet," Jim said. Butler lifted his hat, scratched his head, reset his hat. "Got some business to take care of?" The stitches in Jim's left side pulled and stung when he swung the saddle up onto the horse's back. "Yeah," he answered, trying not to wince. He tied the saddlebags and blanket roll back of the cantleboard, turned the horse around twice, then mounted. "I might be back." Butler watched him ride away.

It was good to be horseback again, and Jim urged the roan horse into a trot. He followed the creek to the east side of town, crossed the wooden bridge, and reined the horse toward a nearly new frame house. He guessed, from what he'd been told, that this was the Tuttle place. The woman who came to the door watched him warily as he approached. Without dismounting, Jim touched his hat brim, and said, "Excuse me, ma'am, would this be the Tuttle residence?"

The woman snapped. "Yes, it is. And you're the Waggoner boy, aren't you"

"Yes, ma'am. I don't suppose Mr. Tuttle is here?"

"No, he is not."

"Would you be Mrs. Tuttle?"

"Yes, I am."

"Thank you, ma'am." Jim turned the horse around and rode away, going around the bridge, splashing across the creek. He forced himself to look straight ahead when he rode past The Tree and the Waggoner dugout, and kept going until he came to the wagon crossing. Riding at a slow, careful walk, his eyes searching everything, Jim came to the Bar W ranch. Away to the north, iron rails ran west to Denver and east all the way to Kansas City and beyond.

He could remember when the Bar W house was nothing more than a sod shack with a sod pen for horses and a sod shed for a stock shelter. Now a big two-story house stood here. It needed paint, but Jim could see that it was well-built and was once somebody's pride and joy. A big shed built of planks sat where a sod shed had once sat, and another smaller shed, also built of planks sat near it. The four wooden corrals looked strong enough to hold a herd of elephants. There were wagons and a buggy, and there was one horse in a corral.

No human was in sight as Jim rode into the ranch yard, but looking to the north he saw four riders coming. He stayed on his horse and waited. When they came closer he recognized Case and one other rider. Whitfield wasn't with them. They came at a trot until they saw Jim, then they pulled their horses down to a walk. Jim waited.

"What the hell do you want?" Case said, reining up in front of Jim. His lantern-jawed face was hard and his eyes were slits. "You ain't got no business here." He dismounted and stood in front of Jim, his hand near the butt of the sixgun he wore.

Jim stayed on his horse. It would have been bad manners to dismount without being invited to. Yet,

126

he knew that in a gunfight being on a horse put him at a disadvantage. The horse could booger at a sudden movement and spoil his aim.

But he'd come here for a purpose and he wasn't ready to leave.

Chapter Twenty-three

Remembering gunshots in the dark and his stolen money, Jim's mood wasn't any friendlier than Case's. "I didn't come here to look at your ugly mug. I came to see Ray Whitfield."

"He ain't here and he don't wanta see you nohow, so just turn that horse around and git."

Jim mulled that over, then said, "Tell him I want to see him. I don't know where I'll be, but everybody knows everybody's business around here and I won't be hard to find."

"Maybe you better make yourself hard to find."

"What if I don't?"

"Then we'll bury you."

Jim couldn't keep a sneer out of his voice. "You by yourself, or do you think you'll need some help?"

"I don't—" Then Case remembered how fast Jim had once drawn that Army Colt and he looked around at the other men, trying to decide what to do.

All heads swiveled toward the house when a man yelled, "Hey!" It was Whitfield, coming toward them, half-running. "Hey!" He came up, breathless, looked at Jim, looked at Case, and said, "I don't . . . know what this is all about, but I don't . . . want no shooting."

Jim said, "I didn't come here to do any shooting, but I damned sure will if any of your hired help reaches for a gun."

"What did you come here for?" The rancher's thin-lipped mouth was tight under the gray mustache.

"I'd like to know more about a trial that took place near here eleven years ago. You were on the jury. I wasn't allowed to watch."

"Yeah, I figured you'd come back here asking about that."

"What did you expect? That I'd just drop off the edge of the world and you'd never see me again? Any objections to telling me about that trial?"

Case said, "Want us to pull 'im off that horse and teach 'im some manners, Ray?"

"No," Whitfield answered quickly. "No, I don't want any trouble." To Jim he said, "There wasn't much to the trial. A man named Prat or Pratts or Pretts testi-fied that two men stampeded his cattle down south on Frenchman's Creek and he found two of his bulls wearing a Running W brand. It was a fresh brand. Your pa and his brother branded a Running W. And what's more, young feller, the Waggoner brothers ad-mitted they branded those bulls."

"Did they admit stealing them?"

"No. Of course not. They knew they'd be hung if they did."

"So you took this Pretts's word."

"Why not? The Waggoners admitted the bulls weren't theirs and they admitted putting their brand on 'em."

"Well." Jim couldn't meet the rancher's gaze. He knew there was more to be learned about the trial, but he didn't know what to ask. Finally, he said, "And this Pretts or whatever his name was identified my dad and my uncle Tobe as the ones who stampeded his cat-tle?"

"That's right."

"He was a liar. They didn't do it."

"What would you have believed?"

Feeling his face getting hot, Jim sputtered, "Can't you . . . can't you tell when a man's lying?"

"Can you?"

Jim had no answer to that. He glanced at Case. Case was wearing a wicked grin. "All right," Jim said, trying to control his frustration, "tell me this: Who claimed the two sections my dad and my uncle claimed?"

"Chester Tuttle bought it when the government offered it for sale."

"Didn't you say you own it?"

"I bought it later from Chester Tuttle."

This was getting nowhere and Jim knew it. Anger and frustration were boiling inside him. He scowled at Case, feeling an urge to say something insulting. Case just sneered. Whitfield spoke again, this time in a calm, easy tone:

"I got no quarrel with you, young feller, and if I was in your place I might be mad too. Now, I won't object if you want to go scratch around in your family dugout and take whatever you find there. But I wish you'd just head on out of here and keep going."

"If you're so damned accommodating," Jim said, "then why in hell did you lock me up in jail and why in hell did you get your hired goons here to try to kill me?"

The rancher's mouth clamped shut for a moment, and he shot a glance at Case. Then he shrugged. "It ain't what it looks like. Case here wasn't acting under my orders. As for locking you up in jail, well, I was hoping you'd get discouraged and leave. I was wrong. Now, will you just drift on?"

"There's more to this," Jim snapped. "There's got to be. I'm not leaving till I find out what it is." With that, he reined his horse around and rode away.

He didn't look back. Whitfield's tone and manner had erased any fear that he'd be shot from behind. But his jaws were clenched as the roan horse splashed

130

across the creek. What had he accomplished? Not one damned thing. Whitfield had an answer for everything. Who else was at that trial? Chester Tuttle, Joe Jamison, and two others he couldn't even remember. Joe Jamison was dead. That left only Tuttle. No, there was another. Pretts.

As he rode back to town, Jim tried to remember Pretts. He was a sodbuster who came from somewhere south. A man wrinkled and hardbitten from a lifetime of fruitless labor. Yeah, it was coming back to Jim now. Pretts rode a mule that he had to keep slapping with a stick. If that was the best he had to ride, no wonder somebody had an easy time running off his cattle. Yeah, he'd ridden up to the dugout one day and said the two brindle bulls were his. Jonathan Waggoner hadn't argued, and had tried to explain why he'd branded the bulls. But Pretts wouldn't listen. He said he'd heard there was a claim court in the territory and he was going to take his complaint to the judge of the court. Still Jonathan Waggoner hadn't argued. He'd even told Pretts where he could find Chester Tuttle.

At supper that night Jonathan and Tobe Waggoner had talked it over and admitted to each other that branding the bulls was a mistake. But, dammit, the bulls had been grazing with their cows for over a year, and if they hadn't branded them, someone else would have. Yet, they admitted again it wasn't smart. They decided they'd try to find this Pretts and help him drive the animals back to where they'd come from. That was what they'd planned to do.

They hadn't had a chance.

Again the mental picture of two dead men swinging from a branch of a big cottonwood came to Jim's mind. For the hundredth time—maybe even the thousandth—he forced it out. He had to think and he couldn't think when he was angry. What to do next? Who to ask questions of? Tuttle? He was the judge and he could remember everything. Or Pretts. Yeah, Pretts was the only witness, the one who'd made the accusations. Exactly what had he told the jury?

Pretts was the one Jim wanted to see.

But was he still alive? And if he was, where was he? Let's see. He came from somewhere south — Frenchman's Creek, Ray Whitfield had said — and he had all the markings of a sodbuster: his lace-up shoes, bib overalls, shapeless hat over his head. And, yeah, he was riding an old U.S. Army saddle with a center-fire rigging. Frenchman's Creek. Jim had heard of the creek, but he didn't know how far south it was. Had to be somewhere this side of the Arkansas River.

"Well, pard," Jim said to the roan horse, "looks like we've got some traveling to do. We'll head south till we come to a creek, then ask everybody we see, and maybe we'll find a gent name of Pretts. Hope he's still alive and hasn't quit the country. Hope he's sociable."

Glancing at the red rim of the western prairie, he added, "Meantime, looks like you'll be cropping the grass for your supper and I'll be sleeping under the stars. Won't be the first time, will it, pard? Won't be the last time either."

He tied the horse to a hitchrail in front of Ma Baker's cafe, loosened the cinches, and went inside. As usual, all motion and conversation ceased the second he came through the door. This was getting old. Dammit, Jim thought, can't a man buy a meal without being stared at like he was some kind of damned freak? He scowled at everyone in the room, then had second thoughts. Turn the other cheek, Mrs. Nance had said. Well, he wouldn't do that, but he'd try to smile. He tried. It was a weak, uncertain kind of smile. But it set the old man in the dirty apron into motion again.

"Yes sir," he said as Jim took a seat at the counter. "We got beef hash, red beans, and sourdough bread — what'll you have?"

With another attempted smile, Jim said, "You wouldn't happen to have any beef hash and beans, would you?"

"Knowed you was a man of good taste." The old man headed for the kitchen to turn in his order. Jim could feel eyes on his back, but he looked straight ahead.

Only a little daylight was left when he mounted the red roan and rode out of town. He went east, crossed the creek, then doubled back west, hoping to fool anyone who might come looking for him. He couldn't stake the horse near the creek. Too many small trees to get the stake rope tangled in. About five miles west of town he found a wide draw with good grass, and dismounted. By the time he had the horse tied to a thirty-foot rope it was dark. He spread his blankets on the ground by feel.

Lying on his back, fully dressed except for his boots, Jim looked up at the stars, listening to his horse graze. He wondered if Janet Carbaugh would be in the store next morning when he went in to buy some chuck. He'd like to get better acquainted with her, but he didn't know how to do it. Aw, he had no business even thinking about her. He had nothing to offer a smart, pretty girl like Janet Carbaugh. Think about something else.

Forcing his mind to switch thoughts was something Jim had had to learn to do over the years. Now he did it again. He wondered if anyone in Apache Wells knew a man named Pretts and where he lived. Who would know? Mrs. Tuttle might know. She hadn't watched the trial, but her husband might have mentioned something to her about Pretts. Would she talk to Jim, the Waggoner boy? She sure hadn't been friendly today when he'd stopped by the Tuttle house. Mrs. Jamison? Maybe. If she'd talk to him again. Janet Carbaugh? Naw. Too young. Her boss, Woodbine? Naw. He wasn't here back then. But Janet Car-

133

baugh knew everyone in town and everyone knew her. Maybe she could find out for him. Naw, he couldn't ask her to do that.

Turning over on his left side, he grunted with pain when the stitches pulled. He turned over on his right side and used his hat for a pillow. Lying there, he decided the only thing he could do was ride south, ask questions — and hope.

Chapter Twenty-four

One of the things Janet Carbaugh liked to do was read the newspapers from Denver that came in on the eastbound. A small bundle of papers was always tossed onto the station platform, and Mr. Woodbine brought it over to the store to sell. He made no profit from them, but they brought people into the store and gave them something to talk about. That's how Janet learned about the attempted murder in Denver.

She was too busy to read the paper herself, and was standing on a stepladder, dusting a high shelf, when a woman customer exclaimed, "Why, Janet, ain't this the Waggoner boy that was hangin' around here?"

"What?" Janet climbed down and looked over the woman's shoulder. She read a headline that said, *THUG CLUBS, STABS CATTLEMAN IN HOTEL.*

Under that a subhead said, *"Cattleman Manages to Shoot, Kill Would-Be Robber."*

The story said: *Violence reared its ugly head at a reputable Denver hotel last night as a visiting cattleman shot and killed an unidentified knife wielder in a hallway. The fatal dispute erupted at the Great Northern Hotel on Larimer Street about two A.M. A hotel guest identified as James Waggoner was treated at Receiving Hospital for a knife wound in his left side and a bruise on the back of his head. He was released from the hospital after treatment, and later left town. Deputy Marshall Owen Fiske related that Mr. Waggoner was awakened by a knock on his hotel room door, and, taking a large caliber pistol in his hand, answered the knock. He was clubbed and stabbed, but managed to fire two shots from the pistol. Both shots hit the hoodlum in the breast and he died instantly. Deputy Fiske reported that he questioned Mr. Waggoner and the hotel night clerk and ascertained that the shooting was in self-defense. Mr. Waggoner was permitted to go on about his business.*

"Oh my," Janet said.

"We all know that young man is nothing but trouble," the woman said. "Ain't that right, Mr. Woodbine."

"Well," Woodbine answered, glancing at Janet, "I, uh, don't know."

"But he's back here," Janet said. "Sheriff Rogers said he came in on the eastbound today. He arrived here just a short time ago, the same time these papers did."

"This is the early edition," Woodbine said. "They sometimes get the early edition on the train and we get to read the news the same day it's printed."

"Then," said Janet, "apparently he wasn't hurt too badly. Now we know where he disappeared to." Silently, she was glad she had learned he was back before she read the newspaper. Otherwise she would have been worried.

"You say he's here again?" The woman's eyebrows were raised. "Why can't he stay away? Why does he keep coming here?"

"Maybe," Janet said, ice in her voice, "if you were in his place you'd do the same." With that, she climbed back on the ladder and resumed dusting.

Early the next morning, Janet saw him again.

He was the first customer at the Apache Wells Mercantile. She hurried to him as soon as he came in the door. "I need to talk to you, Mr. Waggoner. It's important."

"Well, sure, uh, Miss Carbaugh. But I've got to buy some bacon and bread and get on my way."

"On your way? Are you leaving?"

"No. Uh, yeah, but only for a few days. I'm looking

136

for a man name of Pretts, and I think he lives down south on Frenchman's Creek somewhere."

"Pretts?" Janet couldn't keep the surprise out of her voice. "Why, that's the man . . . he's what I need to talk to you about."

"You know him? Do you know where I can find him?"

"Yes, I think so." Glancing around, Janet saw Woodbine counting tins of peaches on a nearby shelf. Woodbine was pretending he didn't hear what was being said, but Janet suspected he didn't miss a word. "Mr. Waggoner, I don't know where we can go to talk, except to my cabin. Can you meet me there at noon?"

"Your cabin? Sure. You say you know where I can find this Pretts?"

"He was here. He took his wife to Denver. She's very sick. He wanted to see you."

"He's looking for me?"

"Yes. You and Chester Tuttle, and he didn't seem to care which of you he found first."

"Well, I was planning on going south today to look for him, but if he's in Denver, then that's where I'll go."

"I'd like a chance to tell you more about what he said to me. It wasn't much, but it might be important."

"Sure. Anything he said might be important. At your cabin? Where is it?"

She told him how to get there, and went back to work. He left. Woodbine came over and put a hand on Janet's shoulder. "Folks are going to talk, you know, you entertaining a young man at your cabin."

"Aw," Janet said, looking down, "let them talk."

He was waiting, sitting cross-legged on the ground near the door when she finally got away from the store. He stood when he saw her coming.

"Come inside, Mr. Waggoner. I have some potato soup that I can warm up for dinner."

He followed her inside, sat in a straight-backed wooden chair, and held his hat in his lap. She noticed how he winced when he used his left had to pull the chair away from the table, and remembered reading that he had been stabbed. "Are you hurt?"

"Naw."

Knowing cowboys, she didn't believe him. "Are you sure? Can I do anything?"

"Naw."

He wouldn't talk about it, she realized, and he was moving around all right. Cowboys believed that if a man could move both arms and legs he wasn't hurt. She built a fire in the small stove and put a pot of soup over an open flame. Glancing at him, she could see by the way he was gripping his hat and avoiding her eyes that he was nervous at being alone in a small cabin with a young woman. Obviously he wasn't accustomed to that. Smiling, she said, "It won't take long. Are you keeping your horse at Butler's barn?"

"Yeah, uh, yes. If I'm going back to Denver I have to leave him there."

"It was no surprise to me that the message from Texas proved you to be the rightful owner of the horse. I got my fifty dollars bond back from the sheriff and I'll give it to you." She reached for a tin can on a high shelf beside the stove, took out the fifty-dollar bill Jim had given her, and handed it to him.

While the soup warmed, she sat in the only other chair in the room. He waited for her to speak again, turning his hat in his hands. She asked, "Do you know who Lowell Pretts is?"

"Yes, Miss—"

She interrupted, "Janet."

"Yes, Janet. I went out to the Bar W yesterday as soon as I got back and Ray Whitfield told me about Pretts."

"He did?" Her eyebrows went up. "Then you know he was the star witness at your father's trial."

"Yes. I don't remember him very well, but I do remember he was the man who said he owned two bulls my dad and uncle branded."

"That's what he told me."

"Did he tell you what he wants to see me about?"

"No. He was mysterious about that. But it's obvious he knows something about the trial that is not common knowledge. Also, he wants to be paid for telling what he knows. I . . . get the impression he's not a man of high principles."

Chuckling without mirth, Jim said, "That's obvious, all right. If he testified in the trial that my dad and Uncle Tobe ran off his cattle, he was lying in his teeth."

Again, Janet's eyebrows went up. "He did that? That's not what he told me. Who told you that?"

"Ray Whitfield."

She gasped "Why . . . Why, he told me he did not identify the men who stole his cattle, and could only say he saw two men. He said he did not identify your father and uncle."

"What?" Now Jim's eyebrows went up. "Ray Whitfield told me just yesterday that this Pretts pointed out my dad and uncle as the two who stampeded his cattle."

"Oh, my. Pretts lied. Someone lied." She clasped her hands tightly in her lap. "This is a good indication, Mr. Waggoner, that someone lied at the trial."

"Jim. Or James. And yeah, somebody sure lied."

"How . . . It's really none of my business, but how did your father and uncle come by those two bulls?"

Shrugging, Jim said, "They just showed up. My uncle Tobe found them grazing with our cows. We didn't know where they came from. Oh yeah, I remember now, they had yoke marks on their necks and shoulders. We figured they were somebody's work bulls that got loose somehow. We just left them alone."

"You didn't brand them immediately?"

"No. We . . . They were a good breed—better, beefier—than our longhorns, and my dad and uncle were glad to have them. But we didn't brand them until a year or more after they showed up. We figured that if anybody was looking for them, they would have found them by then." His mouth turned sour. "Wouldn't you know it, a week after we branded them, this Pretts came riding up on a mule and said they were his. We didn't argue. If they were his, he could have them."

"So your father and uncle didn't steal them at all?"

"No. Maybe it was a mistake to brand them. I don't know. In Texas, where we came from, there were thousands of stray cattle and nobody knew who all of them belonged to. They belonged to whoever caught and branded them. My dad and Uncle Tobe gathered a hundred cows and a few bulls that way and we drove them up here."

"Oh." Janet jumped up. "The soup. I forgot about the soup." Quickly, she wrapped a clean flour sack around her hand and lifted the steaming pot off the stove. "Oh, I hope it isn't burned."

"Sure smells good," Jim said.

"We'll have to let it cool awhile, and if it's not edible I have some fresh bread and plum preserves we can make a meal out of. I apologize, James. I wanted to serve you a hot dinner."

"I appreciate it."

She sat again. "So, I suppose you'll go to Denver and try to find Lowell Pretts and get him to tell the truth about everything."

"Seems like a good plan."

"Yes, but . . ." She paused, thinking, "What if he finds Chester Tuttle first? He indicated he'd sell information to whoever . . . You know, James, he said he knew something that you'd like to know and that Mr. Tuttle wouldn't want known. Oh, and he said Mr. Tuttle owes him. What does that sound like to you?"

"It sounds like he lied at the trial and Chester Tuttle knew he was lying."

"Yes. But also . . ." Her brow wrinkled in a frown. "He lied at the trial and he lied to me. Can we . . . can you believe anything he says? And he wants to be paid.

He's the kind that would say anything for money. I mentioned that his wife is very sick, didn't I? He needs money, no doubt about that."

With a wry smile, Jim said, "I've got a few bucks, but not as much as Chester Tuttle. I hope he ain't taking bids."

Chapter Twenty-five

The soup was scalding hot, but good. Jim had an urge to blow on it to cool it, but his mother, and Mrs. Nance too, had taught him better manners. He also had an urge to do what Zack Dawson often did — fan it with his hat. Instead, he sipped at it until it cooled enough that he could eat it a spoonful at a time. Janet Carbaugh could cook. And pretty? Stealing glances at her, Jim decided she was the prettiest girl he'd ever seen. Her slim, tight little figure, her oval face, and firm chin. Her mouth was perfect — straight with enough lip to mark her as female but not too much. If he could see nothing more of her than her mouth, he'd know she was a pretty young woman. And her big expressive brown eyes. He felt that he could swim in them. She was calling him James and insisting that he call her Janet. He liked that.

Yeah, he sure liked that.

The westbound wouldn't come through Apache Wells until around ten o'clock that night. Janet invited him to come back for supper. He hesitated. "Folks here seem to know everybody else's business, and some folks seem to think I'm a hoodlum, and . . ."

"I know. I refuse to worry about it." She smiled. "Maybe it will keep you out of trouble."

Grinning with her, he said, "It'll sure beat hanging around the saloon."

But he still had time to kill. He went to Butler's barn,

made sure his horse was contented, went for a walk along the creek, saw that he was nearing The Tree, and turned back. When he proved to everyone that his dad and Uncle Tobe were innocent, he'd try again to find their graves and put up a monument of some kind. Maybe he'd get a stone mason in Denver to chisel a message on a big chunk of that mountain granite. Let's see, what should the message say? Something like, "Jonathan Waggoner Tobe Waggoner Innocent Men Hung by Mistake." Something like that.

But old Whitfield owned this land now. Would he allow a monument here? It would remind him, every time he came by here, that he was a party to hanging two innocent men. Maybe, when the truth finally came out, the people of Apache County would want the monument bad enough to make him allow it. If he didn't allow it, he'd be the most unpopular man in Apache County. And old Tuttle, if he'd done anything dishonest and the truth was known, his career as a politician would be over. In fact, if everyone knew about his double life, his career would be over.

Huh. Jim grinned when he thought about it. He could get his revenge on Chester Tuttle without firing a shot. All he had to do was spread the word about the territorial councilman's beautiful redheaded second wife in Denver while his older, plainer wife stayed at Apache Wells. It would be easy. Just tip off the Denver newspaper.

But, aw hell, Jim wasn't the kind to tell tales out of school. Just the same, that goddamn Tuttle had better admit the truth about the trial.

He waited until just after dark to knock on her cabin door. She was expecting him. She wore a clean white apron over her long dress, and her hair had been combed until it formed a lovely frame for her oval face. Something that smelled delicious was cooking on the stove.

"Some fresh beefsteaks came on the eastbound with some other groceries that Mr. Woodbine had ordered, and I bought two of them. How does steak, mashed potatoes, and gravy sound to you?"

"There's nothing I'd like better," Jim said. He accepted her invitation to sit. Still nervous about being here alone with her, his hands crushed his hat, straightened it, and crushed it again. She handed him a folded newspaper.

"Have you read about yourself? You had a very narrow escape in Denver."

"What? That's in the newspaper?"

"Yes, it is. The newspaper found out what happened, but they don't know much about you."

"Well, I'll be darned." He opened the paper, turned pages until he came to the story. He read it, then looked up. "I never thought I'd ever have my name in the papers. I wish it was about something else."

"Apparently the reporter didn't talk to you."

"No, I didn't stay around. I got out of town as fast as I could." He didn't tell her that he suspected the dead man had murder on his mind, and he didn't — oh boy, that reminded him. If it was supposed to be murder for hire, there could be only one explanation for it. And now that he had reason to believe some lying had been done at the trial eleven years ago, the explanation was simple. But he didn't tell her that. Instead he idly looked over the opposite page of the newspaper. An ad printed in large type proclaimed that The Greatest Medical Discovery of the Ages would cure everything from pimples to piles.

"You have a wound in your left side, don't you?"

"Huh? Oh, not much of a wound."

"Are you going back to the doctor?"

"Yeah. Sometime."

She frowned at him a moment, then asked, "How do you like your steak, James? Rare, medium, or well-done?"

"Huh? Oh, medium."

"Me too."

He watched her mash the boiled potatoes with a small kitchen tool that Mrs. Nance had called a spud smasher. That done, she pan-fried the steaks and used the leavings

144

in the skillet to make gravy. When they sat at the table, he half-expected her to ask him to give thanks, and was relieved when she didn't. They ate silently, mainly because that was the way he was accustomed to eating, and also because he didn't know what to say. She seemed comfortable with his silence, and he was grateful.

While she washed dishes and he wiped them dry with a clean muslin towel, she asked him about the people who'd taken him along after the hanging. He told her all about them, and he told her about the Nances on the Double O. He told her a lot about himself. But not everything. She listened, very much interested. Then she told him about going to school in Denver and planning to go back. She would get all the education she could, she said, and then teach school, probably here in Apache Wells. She didn't tell him everything either.

And later, while he rode the swaying, rackety passenger car to Denver, his saddlebags under the seat, he realized she hadn't told him about her childhood. In fact, she knew more about him than he knew about her. Oh well, if she wanted him to know, she'd tell him. He hoped she would one day.

Meanwhile, he had other things to learn.

He stayed away from the Great Northern Hotel, not wanting to talk to anyone about the shooting in the hotel hall, and instead checked into the Grant Hotel on Market Street. After riding the passenger car all night he was tired and dirty but, carrying his saddlebags, he wasted no time in finding the Receiving Hospital. When he asked for a patient named Pretts, he was directed to a ward containing about twenty beds. A nurse pointed to a bed against a far wall. A middle-aged woman was lying there on her side with her mouth open and her eyes half-open. She was breathing in noisy gasps. He didn't bother her. Outside the ward, in a hall on a wooden bench, a man in bib overalls sat with his face in his hands. He was bald on

145

top, with gray whiskers. A floppy black hat lay on the floor beside the bench. Jim approached him.

"Pardon me, are you Lowell Pretts?"

The man looked up. His face was strained, haggard. "I'm him."

"My name is James Waggoner. I've been told you were looking for me."

"Huh? Oh." The weary face showed some life. "Yeah, I was lookin' fer you at Apache Wells."

Sitting beside him on the wooden bench, Jim said, "I was told you were a witness at a trial eleven years ago on Apache Creek. My dad and uncle were hung after that trial."

"Yeah, I was, but . . ." The face took on a wary look. "I didn't have nothin' to do with no hangin'. I only told the jury about my bullocks bein' stole."

"Did you point out my dad and uncle as the ones who stole them?"

"I, uh, I need money awful bad. My wife is in there and she's so sick she don't even know me anymore. Diphtheria, the doctor said."

Jim was silent a moment. He watched two men with short-trimmed beards and white coats go into the ward. Then, mouth tight, he said, "Yeah, I heard you have to be paid to tell the truth."

"I need money awful bad."

"How about fifty dollars?"

"I gotta have more'n that. The doctor wants sixty for hisself and the hospital wants twenty bucks a day. And I ain't had no sleep for three, four days. And there's medicine to pay for."

Feeling a little pity now, Jim said, "All right, a hundred. But you'll have to tell the truth to a judge, or somebody important."

"If I had a hundred and fifty, I could see she's moved to a better room and gets a nurse to watch over her all the time."

With a sigh, Jim said, "All right. I've got a hundred and

146

fifty in paper money."

"You give it to me and I'll tell all about that trial to anybody you want me to tell it to."

Jim reached for his bankroll, pulled it out of a shirt pocket, untied the string. But before he could count out the money, one of the men in white came out of the ward. "Mr. Pretts?"

The man looked at him, fear and dread written all over his face.

"I'm sorry to have to tell you, Mrs. Pretts just passed away."

A long pitiable groan rose from Pretts. He buried his face in his hands. Jim sat beside him, not knowing what to say or do. He peeled three fifty-dollar bills from his roll, and tried to press them into Pretts's hand.

"It don't matter now," Pretts groaned. He looked up at the man in white. "I wanta see her. Can I see her now?"

"Yes, of course."

Jim tried again to hand over the money, but the man shook his head. "It don't matter now."

"Take it. It'll see she has the right kind of burial." He put the money in Pretts's shirt pocket. "I'm staying at the Grant Hotel on Market Street, Mr. Pretts. When you feel like it, come and talk to me."

The man in baggy overalls stood, picked up his hat, and headed with unsteady steps toward the ward door. Jim turned, and, looking down, walked out of the hospital.

Back at his hotel, Jim shaved and took a bath in a tin tub. He ate in a workingman's cafe, bought a newspaper, and went back to his room. There, he read awhile, but saw nothing interesting. He pulled his boots off and lay back on the bed. As tired as he was, he couldn't get Pretts out of his mind. The man's wife had just died. He couldn't get information out of a man whose wife had just died. Dammit. Well, he'd have to wait. Maybe Pretts would come knocking on his hotel-room door. Maybe not.

No, he couldn't just lie here in this little room and wait.

He'd give Pretts a few hours and go find him. He shouldn't be hard to find. With that plan in mind, Jim fell asleep.

At midafternoon, traffic noise from the street awakened him. Heavy wagon wheels rumbled, trace chains rattled, teamsters yelled. Damned city racket would wake up the dead. He poured water from a pitcher into a bowl and washed his face. Then he ate in the same cafe he had before and walked to the hospital.

Mr. Pretts had had his wife's body moved to the Cherry Creek Mortuary, he was told. He was told where the mortuary was. He walked the ten blocks, wishing he had a horse. Inside a low brick building, he found a tall man in a swallowtail black coat, rearranging plush satin pillows on a row of benches. A pulpit stood in front of the benches. A six foot-high cross was fastened to a wall behind the pulpit. No caskets were in sight, but Jim could see through a door into a back room, and he guessed that that was where the bodies were. The tall man wore wire-framed glasses low on his nose and a solemn expression on his face. The place smelled something like strong horse liniment, only worse.

"Yes, Mrs. Pretts is here, but she will not lie in state," he said. "However, Mr. Pretts arranged for a very nice memorial service. Burial will be in Evergreen Cemetery tomorrow morning. Are you a relative, sir?"

"No," Jim said quickly. "I . . . I'm an acquaintance of Mr. Pretts. Would you happen to know where he's staying?"

"No, sir, I do not. He said he is from out of town and had not found a place to stay. When he left, he said he would find a hotel and come back."

Nothing to do but wait. No, he couldn't wait here. This place smelled god-awful, the atmosphere was god-awful, and it was no place to wait. The funeral was tomorrow morning. All right, he'd come back tomorrow morning. He wanted no part of a memorial service or a funeral, but he had to talk to Lowell Pretts. No, dammit, a funeral was no place to ask questions. Well, he could at least ask the bereaved where he was staying, and talk to him later. Yeah, he could do that much.

Time to kill. A warm beer in a saloon. Read more of the Daily Rocky Mountain News. Read a headline that said, *Telegraph*, and a stack of subheads under that. They said, *Midnight Dispatches Are there any Ku-Klux Investigations before the Congressional Subcommittee?* What in hell was the Ku-Klux? A poorly cooked meal in the working man's cafe. Another warm beer. A shot of whiskey. Ga-a-a-h. A proposition from a woman with a worn-out face and sagging shoulders. A restless night in a too-soft hotel bed, wondering what Lowell Pretts would have to say, trying to think of who he could get to witness what Lowell Pretts had to say, wishing he knew more about the law. Thinking of Janet Carbaugh. Daylight was a relief.

He was at the mortuary early, before the memorial service had begun. The big room with the pulpit and cross was empty. He walked across the wooden floor, purposely stomping hard, hoping to attract attention. It worked.

"Yes, sir?" It was the tall man in the black swallowtail coat coming through the connecting door. "You are the gentleman who was here last evening, are you not?"

"Yes, I—"

"And you were asking about a Mr. Lowell Pretts?"

"Yes. I need to talk to him for a second. Only for a second."

"I'm afraid you are too late, sir."

"What? I thought the service was going to be this morning."

"It has been rescheduled, sir. It will be a double service and burial."

"What?" Jim said again, flabbergasted. "I don't understand."

"Mr. Pretts has followed his beloved wife into the hereafter."

Jim couldn't believe what he was hearing. "Huh?"

149

"Yes, sir. His body was just brought in. He is not ready for viewing yet, sir. If you would care to come back in about an hour . . ."

"What happened?"

"He is the victim of a gunshot, sir. The police believe it was self-inflicted."

Chapter Twenty-six

What now, James B. Waggoner? he asked himself as he walked to Market Street and the Grant Hotel. The trip to Denver had all been for nothing. The one hundred fifty dollars might as well have been wadded up and tossed into Cherry Creek. All it had done was keep the Prettses from being buried in paupers' graves. What did he owe them?

Feeling bitter, he walked, head down, seeing no one. Go get your horse and outfit from Butler's barn, say good-bye to Janet Carbaugh, and drift. That's what everybody wants. Get rid of the Waggoner boy before he goes crazy and kills somebody. As the sheriff said, he's trouble looking for a place to happen. As Zack Dawson said, he could shoot holes in somebody for revenge, but all that would get him was a hangman's noose for himself.

Put it behind you, James B. Waggoner. You got what you came to Colorado Territory for. Drift.

Yeah, he had what he'd come for, and more. What more? Well, he'd learned more about that trial eleven years ago. What? He'd learned that somebody lied. And that wasn't all. Somebody wanted him either long gone or dead. Preferably dead. Why? Because of the lie. Not only that, the main witness at the trial was now dead. Suicide? Maybe. Maybe not.

Lowell Pretts had told Janet Carbaugh he knew

something that James Waggoner would like to know and would be willing to pay for. And it was something that Chester Tuttle would pay him to keep quiet about. That something was The Lie. What lie? Who lied?

Tuttle knew.

Where to find Chester Tuttle? Councilman Tuttle. His wife, his new wife, had said he had an office next door to the territorial capitol. Where was the capitol?

"Sir," Jim said to a passing man in business clothes, "could you direct me to the capitol building?"

It was near Cherry Creek, not far from the mortuary, a two-story brick building with a red tile roof. On the corner, in the same city block, was a small frame building with a sign on a post in front that said, LAW OFFICES Under those two words was painted, THE HONORABLE CHESTER C. TUTTLE COUNCILMAN.

Inside, Jim found himself in a short hall with two doors on each side. He opened an office door, looked in at clerks, both men and women, bent over desks, and asked where he could find Councilman Tuttle. On the other end of the hall, opposite side, he was told. Of course. Tuttle's name was painted in black on a frosted-glass window. Jim opened that door.

It was Chester Tuttle, all right, with his round red face, sitting behind a big desk with a younger man in a boiled white shirt in a straight chair on his right. The young man was writing in a notebook while Tuttle talked. Both men stopped what they were doing and looked up as Jim opened the door.

"Pardon me," Jim said, "you're Chester Tuttle, aren't you?"

"Yes, sir, I am," the politician answered.

Jim came on into the room. Both men waited for him to say more. "You don't recognize me, do you, Mr. Tuttle."

"I'm, uh, afraid I don't."

"My name is Waggoner. James B. Waggoner. Son of Jonathan Waggoner."

152

The politician's mouth opened as understanding came across his face. "Why, yes. I recognize the name."

"I'd like to talk to you."

"Of course. Are you a resident of the territory? I am always more than happy to talk to one of my constituents."

"I'm not one of your constituents. I'm the son of a man you hung eleven years ago."

Tuttle had to clear his throat. He glanced at the young clerk, then met Jim's gaze. "I, uh, suppose you would like to learn all about the trial in which a Mr. Jonathan Waggoner and a Mr. Tobe Waggoner were found guilty of cattle stealing."

"Yes, sir. That is why I'm here."

"Well, sir, I will be happy to tell you everything. I realize that you were very young at the time and probably do not recall all the details."

"I wasn't allowed at the trial."

"Of course you weren't. For the sake of decorum, children were excluded from the proceedings."

"All right, I'm not a child now, and I want to know all about it."

Clearing his throat again, Tuttle said, "Mr. Waggoner, I hope you didn't come here seeking revenge. The trial was conducted in a perfectly proper manner, and the evidence was conclusive. We did what we had to do."

Jim could feel it slipping away from him. This was turning out the same as his conversation with Ray Whitfield. Everything that happened back then was proper. Jim knew better. But he didn't know what to say next. "I, uh . . ." Aw, hell, he told himself, quit trying to be polite and say it outright. "Mr. Tuttle, that trial was not a fair trial. Somebody lied."

Instead of showing shock or surprise, the politician's face softened, his shoulders slumped, and he shook his head sadly. "I'm sorry you feel that way, Mr. Waggoner. I can't imagine why you would believe that."

153

"Remember Lowell Pretts?"

Still no change in Tuttle's expression. "Of course. Lowell Pretts was the victim of the theft. He was our main witness."

"Exactly what did he say in the trial?"

"I remember it all very well. After all, it was the only time I ever had to order an execution. It was a very hard decision to make. But under the circumstances, I had no choice."

"What did Lowell Pretts say?"

"He testified under oath that two men stole some cattle from him. They just ran off the cattle and fired several shots at him when he tried to go in pursuit. Later he found two of his cattle, two brindle bulls, grazing with a herd belonging to the Waggoner brothers. The bulls had been recently branded with the Waggoners' brand." Tuttle leaned back in his chair, and put his fingertips under his chin, apparently searching his memory. The young clerk looked from Tuttle to Jim. Tuttle added, "One of the brothers testified that they did indeed brand the bulls."

"Is that all he said? Did he tell the jury how long the bulls had been grazing with our cows before we branded them?"

"No, uh, I believe not. Or . . . yes. Yes, he did testify that the bulls appeared one day about a year earlier. He said he did not know where they came from."

"And the jury didn't believe him?"

"Obviously not. Which is understandable. After all, Mr. Pretts did positively identify the Waggoner brothers as the men who stole his cattle."

Jim had a powerful urge to yell, "Liar, liar," but he didn't. It would have accomplished nothing. Instead, he asked, "Did you know that Lowell Pretts is here in Denver?"

At that, the politician's hands came down and rested on the desk. "He is? Have you talked to him?"

"Yes, I have."

"Did he—Then, he surely verified what I just told you."

"No, he didn't."

"Are you telling me, Mr. Waggoner, that Lowell Pretts recanted his testimony?"

"Recanted? Uh, no. He did say he knew something about the trial that I would like to know. He offered to sell me information."

"What information?"

Yeah, it was slipping away. He had no information. Or—come to think of it: "Lowell Pretts said he did not identify my dad and my uncle as the men who stole his cattle. He said he testified that they could have been. You said, just now, that he positively identified them."

Chester Tuttle's forehead wrinkled and he hesitated before saying more. Then, "If that is what he told you, then you're right, he was lying. Whether he lied to you or to the jury is something we will have to determine. I want to have a talk with Mr. Lowell Pretts. Would you be so kind as to tell me where he is to be found?"

"He's dead."

This time shock did appear on the politician's face. "Dead? How, when, here in Denver?"

"His wife died yesterday at Receiving Hospital. The undertaker said Pretts was found dead this morning, and the police think he shot himself."

"Oh, my God. How terrible." A pause, then, "But before he died, he told you he did not identify the Waggoner brothers as the men who stole his cattle."

Jim had to look down. "He didn't tell me anything. He said that to a young lady in Apache Wells. He told her he wanted to tell me something, but he had to bring his wife to the hospital. That's why I'm in Denver."

"Oh, I see. Then he told his story to a third person. Did he say the same thing to anyone else?"

"I doubt it."

"What exactly did he say to this . . . this mysterious third person?"

"I wasn't there."

The politician pondered that, frowning. "And you said he wanted money for the information?"

"Yes. He needed money to pay the doctor and the hospital."

Another negative shake of the head. "Then, it appears, Mr. Waggoner, that Lowell Pretts was trying to raise money and was willing to lie to do it. I believe he told the truth at the trial and lied to the young woman. By the way, who is the young woman?"

Now Jim shook his head. "She might not appreciate being brought into this."

Leaning back in his chair again, Councilman Tuttle laced his fingers across his brocaded vest. "I wish I could say or do something to make you feel better about everything, Mr. Waggoner. You're young. Do not let an event that took place eleven years ago cloud your life. How I wish I were young like you again."

He'd lost. He was outtalked, outslicked, and outsmarted. He could feel the frustration burning his face, the stitches pulling in his left side. Chester Tuttle was looking at him sympathetically. The clerk was smirking, exactly the way Case had smirked at him. He had to do something, say something.

"Just the same . . . I was ten years old, old enough to know what was going on. My dad and my uncle did not lie. Somebody else lied. Either Lowell Pretts, or Ray Whitfield, or . . . or you."

That got a reaction. Chester Tuttle stood so suddenly, he knocked his chair over. "Are you calling me a liar, young man?"

"Somebody is a lair. And I'll tell you something else, somebody tried to kill me. Not once but three times. And I've got a suspicion Lowell Pretts was murdered. I know something damned strange went on eleven years ago, and I, by God, aim to find out what."

Outside, the sky was dark and threatening over the mountains to the west while a bright sun shone overhead. Jim walked, head down, not seeing, not hearing, the sights and sounds of the city. So he aimed to find out. Yeah, sure. Big words. Words spoken in anger and frustration. He'd made an ass of himself. Chester Tuttle was laughing up his sleeve. For the second time in as many days, he asked himself:

What now?

The main witness was dead. One of the jurors was dead and two others were gone. He'd already questioned the other juror, Ray Whitfield, and he'd questioned the judge. There was no one left to question.

Except Mrs. Tuttle. She was married to the judge, slept with him, ate with him.

But she wouldn't talk to Jim.

As far as most folks in Apache Wells were concerned, Jim was a troublemaker. And hell, maybe he was. If he could prove that somebody lied at the trial, he'd sure as hell make trouble. Some-damn-body would sure as hell pay.

Would Janet Carbaugh question Mrs. Tuttle for him? Or would that be asking too much of her? Well, he had to go back to Apache Wells anyway to get his horse and saddle. If Janet didn't want to help, he'd . . . what? Try to find one of the other jurors. It might be impossible, but there was nothing left to do but try. Now that he knew for sure that somebody had lied eleven years ago, he intended to find out who and why. And prove it to every-damn-body in Colorado Territory.

And then he'd erect that monument.

Chapter Twenty-seven

It was Postum Cereal Food Coffee the woman wanted, and Janet had to apologize for not having any.

"Coffee is an evil brew," the woman said. "It's a destroyer of health. Mr. Postum should be rewarded for inventing a hot drink that's made out of grains grown right here in the good old U.S. of A." She was a youngish woman whom Janet knew as Mrs. Oscar Williams. The Williamses ran a hundred head or so of bony longhorn cattle somewhere west of Apache Wells. They had two boys around twelve years old.

"We've heard of Postum's cereal," Janet said, "but we haven't been able to order any. However, we do have two boxes of Osborn's Celebrated Java. Folks who have tried it have come back for more."

"Not for me and my boys. Why, that's worse than alcohol."

Janet saw her stepfather come in, but all she could do was nod and say, "Good morning." Ray Whitfield waited patiently.

Janet finally sold the woman a month's supply of flour, sugar, baking soda, dried fruit, and cured ham. The woman settled for one foil-wrapped packet of Java, and a sack of fake coffee made of grain, ground nutshells, and chicory. "The Java's for my husband," Mrs. Williams explained. "I keep telling him he's ruining his health, but . . ." She rolled her eyes upward. Janet thought it best not to comment.

There were two other customers to wait on, and finally she had time to speak to her stepfather. "I want to ask you about the trial, you know, eleven years ago, but I don't have time now. Can you come to my house at noon? I'll fix something to eat."

"Well, I'd sure like to, Janet, but I've got work to do. Besides, don't know anymore about that trial than you've already heard."

Glancing at a woman who came through the door, Janet said hastily, "There was a Mr. Pretts here. Lowell Pretts. He said something that I'd like to ask you about."

"Lowell Pretts? He's here?"

"He was. He's gone to Denver now." Turning to the newly-arrived customer, Janet said, "Good morning, Mrs. Jamison. I'll be right there." To Ray Whitfield, she said, "It's important."

Whitfield frowned. "All right. At noon."

It was a busy morning, and Janet was relieved when Woodbine, her boss, told her to go on home and eat. Whitfield wasn't there, but he showed up shortly after she'd built a fire in the stove and put some soup on to warm. Knowing that cattlemen and cowboys usually ate in silence, she waited until her stepfather had consumed two bowls of bean-and-sausage soup and two thick slices of bread before she asked bluntly:

"What did Lowell Pretts say at the trial? Did he positively identify the Waggoner brothers as the men who stole his cattle?"

"Why, yes." Whitfield scooted his chair away from the table and crossed his legs. "Why are you so interested, Janet? It was a long time ago. Why don't you just forget it?"

"So it was a long time ago. It hasn't been forgotten. It's very important for—" All right, why not admit it? "Ever since I heard the story, I have sympathized with the Waggoner boy. He came back here after eleven years, not to shoot anyone, but to try to clear his father's name. I'm

159

beginning to believe his father and uncle were not the thieves they were made out to be."

"Why would you believe that?"

"The things that happened after the hanging, and—"

He interrupted, face red, "What things?"

"The Waggoners' claim was right between land claimed by you and Chester Tuttle and—"

Ray Whitfield stood so quickly he bumped the table and rattled the dishes. "Are you accusing me and Chet Tuttle of something? Are you?" His face was red and his voice was shaking. "Why would you accuse your own stepdad of anything? Didn't I treat you and your mother right? Didn't I give you some cows so you could build your own herd. Why in hell are you accusing me of anything?"

Suddenly, she felt like apologizing. "It's . . . really, that's not what's got me curious, it's something Lowell Pretts said. He said he did not positively identify the Waggoner brothers as the men who stole his cattle."

"He said that? When did he say that?"

"Why, just two days ago. He was here, on his way to Denver. His wife is very sick, and he took her to Denver on the train."

"What else did he say?"

"That's about all. He was mysterious."

"The hell he was." Today was the first time Janet had heard her stepfather swear. "Just who all did he say that to?"

"As far as I know, just me. But he was looking for Mr. Tuttle, and when he couldn't find him he asked about James Waggoner. He said he wanted to sell them some information about the trial. He needed money."

"Why, that weak-livered, pasty-faced little . . . He went to Denver, you say?"

"Yes."

"You seem to know so much about the Waggoner boy, where is he right now?"

"He went to Denver to find Lowell Pretts. He should know by now what Mr. Pretts has to say."

160

"Is that so?" The rancher was suddenly pensive. "You say Pretts took his wife to a hospital?"

Janet nodded.

"When did Waggoner go to Denver?"

"Last night." Then a thought popped into Janet's head. "Why did you call Lowell Pretts weak-livered? Is he a weakling?"

"Why, uh." And then the rancher gathered his wits. "If he said one thing at the trial and another thing to you eleven years later, he's worse than weak-livered."

"Is it possible that he lied at the trial?"

"No." Whitfield clamped his hat on his head. "Not likely. You say he needed money? Some men will say anything for money." He stomped out of the house to a horse tied at a hitching post. Janet watched him swing into the saddle. "Mighty good soup," the rancher said, and rode away at a lope.

"Yes," Janet said to his back as he rode away, "some people will say anything for money."

He couldn't get a train back to Apache Wells until next morning, and Jim again had time to kill. He went back to the same workingmen's cafe and had a meal of tough boiled beef and fried potatoes. A man in dirty overalls sitting next to him at the counter grumbled, "This meat is tougher'n a boiled owl. My dog couldn't chew this."

Jim nodded in agreement.

Swallowing without chewing his food thoroughly left a lump in his stomach. He bought the morning newspaper, took it to his hotel room, and read everything of interest. Under the headline, *TERRITORIAL NEWS*, was a story about a shooting at Black Hawk. Jim didn't know where Black Hawk was, but he guessed it was a mining town somewhere west of Denver. There were a lot of ads, including one of a dentist who called himself a painless dentist. Not much news. After a bath in a tin tub he wished he had some clean clothes, but decided not to buy any. That hundred and fifty dollars he'd wasted on Lowell Pretts had left a big dent in his bankroll. He went to a bank and changed his gold eagles for paper money. Folding money was lighter and easier to carry. On his way back, he stopped in a saloon for a beer. Feeling lonely, he glanced at the other men at the bar. There were only two. One was so drunk he was about to fall over, and the other was growling at his reflection in the bar mirror. "She shouldn't a said that," he growled. "No sir, it ain't true. I didn't do it. She shouldn't a said that."

At a table near the bar, a man in plaid clothes and a pencil mustache riffled a deck of cards and looked at Jim speculatively. Jim refused to meet his gaze, and recalled more words of advice from Zack Dawson: "You can't beat a man at his own game." Jim never cared much for card games anyway.

Leaving the saloon, he walked down Larimer Street, looking at the merchandise in store windows. A saddle in the window of a harness shop caught his eye. He stopped to study it. Beautiful. The leather was hand-carved in a rose design, and the conchas were made of bright silver. Wouldn't a working cowboy look funny in an outfit like that? Also, the rigging hung under the fenders — a three-quarter rigging — and that would have been snorted at in Texas.

Behind him, a boy yelled: "Evenin' news. First edition. Getcher news here." He wore a ragged bill cap and corduroy pants with holes in the knees, and he carried a stack of newspapers under his left arm. "How much?" Jim asked. "Two cents, mister." Jim gave him a nickel and refused the change.

In his hotel room, he scanned the pages and found what he was looking for on page three: SUICIDE IN DENVER HOTEL

A double tragedy occurred yesterday and early this morning that began in Receiving Hospital and ended in a lonely room at the Great Northern Hotel. At the hospital, a woman identified as Mrs. Margaret Pretts passed on while her husband waited outside the hospital

*ward in the corridor. Then early this morning hotel guests were
awakened by a gunshot coming from the room occupied by her husband Mr. Lowell Pretts. Upon entering the room, authorities
found Mr. Pretts dead and a .22 caliber doubled-barreled derringer
in his hand. Mr. Pretts had died instantly from a bullet wound in
his right temple. Authorities said the death was suicide, apparently
the result of profound despondency. Mr. and Mrs. Pretts will be
buried side by side . . .*

Jim put the paper down, thinking. A .22 caliber derringer? That wasn't the kind of gun a rancher or farmer
would carry. It was a hideout gun, one that could be carried out of sight in a pocket or boot. It wasn't worth a
damn for anything except close-range self-defense. The
Great Northern Hotel? This was the second shooting
death there in a week.

Jim remembered that the desk clerk had fallen asleep
in his chair one night. Maybe he had a habit of doing that.
He didn't know who went up and down those stairs at
night. But a gunshot would have awakened him. He
would have seen who came down. Jim finished reading
the story. Nothing was said about the clerk seeing anything suspicious.

Maybe it was suicide. Maybe Lowell Pretts had used
some of that hundred and fifty bucks to buy a cheap little
gun for the purpose of killing himself. Maybe. Maybe
not.

Jim left the Grant Hotel and headed for the Great
Northern. The desk clerk, a bald man in a striped shirt,
recognized him, but he wasn't the night clerk. No, he
said, he wasn't on duty when one of the guests shot himself.

"Well, I was wondering," Jim said, standing with his
thumbs hooked inside his gunbelt, "I know — knew —
Lowell Pretts, and I was wondering what time of the night
it happened."

"Like I said, I wasn't here, but I heard about it. John,
the night clerk, said he heard the shot early this morning."

"After daylight, or . . ."

"Yeah, it was after daylight. He was making himself some coffee."

"He didn't see anybody come down the stairs after the shot?"

"Nope. He went up to see what he could see and he found a couple of other guests in the hall. They'd heard the shot too and pointed to the room it came from."

"Who was in the room next to Lowell Pretts?"

"I ain't sure I'm s'posed to be telling you all this. The police don't like nobody poking around in their business."

"I knew Lowell Pretts. I came to Denver to talk to him. I had some business with him."

"Oh, well, let's see." He turned the hotel register around to where he could read it. "Mr. Pretts was in room two-oh-six. In two-oh-four was a Mrs. Oswald from Cheyenne, and in room two-oh-eight was a Mr. Thomas C. Harvey. He was from Cheyenne too."

"Did you see this Harvey?"

"Yeah, he checked out this morning, after all the excitement died down. Why?"

"I was wondering if he was anybody I'd recognize. Can you remember what he looks like?"

"A heavyset man. He wore a laborer's clothes. Looked like a miner or railroad worker: Let's see, he, uh—oh yeah, he had on a bowler hat. I remember the hat because it didn't go with the rest of his clothes. No beard. Looked like he'd just shaved. Does that sound like somebody you know?"

Jim had to think about that. Then, "No. I don't know him. I guess he just happened to be in the next room. Does your book show what time he checked in?"

"No. Just the date."

"Well, thanks."

Outside on the street, Jim realized he hadn't learned a thing. Nobody had come down the stairs after the gunshot. That meant Pretts either shot himself, or whoever shot him had been staying in a nearby room. It could have been this Harvey. He could have been sent there to shut

164

Pretts's mouth. It could have been . . .

"Aw, hell," Jim mumbled. A man pedestrian turned and looked at him quizzically as he walked by.

Later that night, Jim saw the man in the bowler hat.

Chapter Twenty-eight

It was restlessness that drove him out of his hotel and onto the streets of Denver. It was restlessness that directed his steps into a drinking and gambling emporium called the Silver Dollar Lounge. Lounge, hell, it was just another saloon with a long bar, gaming tables, wicked pictures on the walls, and over-painted women. Jim ordered a beer at the bar, then turned and looked over the crowd. There were all kinds of men in the room, including a half-dozen cowboys at a table in the corner. They were drinking and talking loud, but minding their own business. Jim remembered being told that cattlemen in the territory drove their beeves to Denver where they could be shipped to eastern markets. He guessed that these gents had just corralled a herd at the railroad stockyards. Two of them noticed him looking them over. He nodded pleasantly. They nodded back.

"Buy me a drink, cowboy?" She was young, not so hard-looking, but wearing a cheap low-cut dress. She was kind of attractive.

Jim didn't want to buy her a drink, but he didn't know how to decline politely. "Well, uh . . ."

Suddenly, she screeched, "What? What did you call me? Why, you cheap piece of cowshit, how dare you call me that!"

Embarrassed, knowing everyone was looking at him, Jim could only sputter, "Why, I didn't . . ."

"You did too! You called me a dirty name. How dare you call me that!"

Another voice put in, a man's voice, ominous, "Better apologize, cowboy." He stood on Jim's left, a fancy dresser with black hair parted in the middle and slicked back. His hands held back the lapels of his finger-length coat, showing a pearl-handled pistol in a low-cut holster. It was strapped to the left side of his chest, butt forward.

"Why," Jim sputtered, "I didn't say—"

"He did too. He called me a dirty name. I don't have to take that kind of insult."

"Are you going to apologize cowboy?" The man's right hand was in position to dart inside the coat and jerk out the pistol.

The surprise had worn off by now, and Jim could see what was happening. He guessed that the pearl-handled gun was one of the new single-action revolvers that fired metallic cartridges and didn't have to be cocked. It would fire as fast as the trigger could be pulled. He believed he could draw and cock his Army Colt as fast as the dandy could draw the smaller gun, and he turned to face him, ready.

Then he felt another man beside him, on his right, close. Close enough to grab his gun hand. Barely turning his head, he got a look at the man, and was shocked. He was husky, in a workingman's clothes, but with a bowler hat. His hands were open, ready to grab.

"Apologize, mister."

Jim tried to step aside, away from the man in the bowler hat. The man moved too, staying right beside him.

They had him. If he tried to draw, Bowler Hat would grab his gun hand and slow him enough that the dandy could draw the pearl-handled gun and shoot him dead-center.

"I'm giving you one more chance," the dandy said.

The girl screeched, "Shoot 'im, Bob. He called me a dirty name. Shoot 'im."

167

Jim's mind raced. He might jump to one side and draw the Army Colt, but it probably wouldn't work. The dandy was no greenhorn. Neither was Bowler Hat. He might twist to face Bowler Hat and shoot him, but it would be his last shot. No other plan came to his mind. There was no use apologizing to the girl. They intended to kill him. He could see it coming, feel it. He was about to die in a dirty saloon in the dirty city of Denver.

Then another man's voice was heard, a slow drawly voice. "Now, if I was you fellers, I'd just stand right still. 'Cause if you plug this here cowhand, we're gonna plug you."

The dandy and Bowler Hat suddenly stiffened. The dandy's hand came away from his gun. Looking around, Jim saw them, the cowboy crew that had been sitting at a table. Five or six of them surrounded him and the two would-be killers.

The dandy was sputtering now, "But . . . but he insulted my girl. I can't let any man do that."

"The hell you beller. We saw and heered the whole show. You're just lookin' fer a chance to show ever'body how good you are with that there popper. Only, you wasn't takin' any chances that some cowhand could maybe outdraw and outshoot you, and you got your shit-eatin' pard here to help you."

"Why . . . why this cowpoke's not one of your crew."

"That's so, but he's one of our breed. We gotta watch one another's backs when we come to Denver. We gotta pertect one another from you skunk-shit city slicks." He turned to the girl. "Excuse my language, ma'am. I shore wouldn't want to insult you."

That got a laugh from everyone in the room. The dandy's face was red. Bowler Hat had his hands down at his sides, looking pale. Jim backed up against the bar and grinned.

"Well . . . well, don't let it happen again." The dandy spun on his heels and walked away. Bowler Hat followed.

Still grinning, Jim said, "You gents sure saved my bacon. Let me buy you a drink."

"Come on over to the table," a cowboy said. "We'll buy you one." Jim went with them, pulled a chair away from another table, and sat. "Where you from?" a cowboy asked.

"West Texas by way of Apache Creek." Jim was still grinning.

"I used ta work in west Texas. What outfit was you with?"

"The Double O. Ever hear of it?"

"Why, hell, yes. Ever'body's heered of the Double O. I hear it's a good outfit. I hear they feed good. What's that feller's name that ramrods it, uh . . ."

"Walls," Jim answered, "George Walls. Wagon boss is a man name of Hudine. Charley Hudine. Good man."

"I'm gonna drift down there purty soon. Before the snow flies in this country. My old bones wasn't made for this Colorado cold. What're you drinkin'?"

Jim had three shots of whiskey and enjoyed visiting with men of his kind. They talked about the climate, the grass, the horses. When he began feeling his liquor, Jim announced, "Well, I've got a soft bed in the Grant Hotel. Think I'll haul my freight over there. Where are you all staying?"

"Some fleatrap over by the stockyards."

Standing, Jim said, "If I ever bump into any of you all again, I'll sure split what I've got with you." He turned to leave.

"Don't take no wooden nickels."

Grinning, Jim said, "Tell you one thing, I'm not gonna even look at another saloon woman."

Sleep was sporadic that night. Jim was worried. Someone wanted him dead and he knew who. How to prove it was something else. But what worried him now was the girl in Apache Wells. Janet Carbaugh. He'd told the wrong man that Lowell Pretts had talked to a young woman in Apache Wells. He hadn't named her, but anyone could go to Apache Wells and learn in five minutes who she was.

Jim had to get back as fast as possible. She didn't know anything about protecting herself.

"My god," he groaned aloud, "did I open my stupid mouth one time too many and put her life in danger too?"

Chapter Twenty-nine

Everyone at Apache Wells heard the eastbound Kansas Pacific coming before it arrived. Janet's boss, Mr. Woodbine, put on his homburg hat, unrolled his shirtsleeves, and prepared to meet it. "I won't need the wagon today," he said to Janet. "I'm not expecting a shipment, and I can carry the mail and the newspapers. Watch the store, will you, please?"

Two customers were checking the shelves to see what had arrived on the latest shipment from the east. Mrs. Chester Tuttle was one of them. "These new airtight cans are dangerous, Janet," she said. "People have got ptomaine poison from eating out of these cans."

"You have to empty them right away after you open them," Janet said.

"It's a handy way to fix a meal, but I want no traffic with anything that gives a body poison."

Janet wrinkled her nose. "I've been told that the canned oysters are very good, but they look disgusting."

"I want no traffic with anything so slimy. I'd as soon eat worms."

"Maybe someone will find a safe way to can food one day. It would save a lot of work for wives and mothers."

"It's too easy," the other woman put in. "Cookin' a good meal takes time, but I'd be ashamed to admit it if I couldn't fix supper for my man without openin' one a them tin cans."

171

"Mrs. Tuttle," Janet said, motioning the older woman aside and speaking apologetically, "I don't want to be a bother, but, you know, Ray Whitfield never discusses business with me — we ladies are not supposed to concern ourselves with men's business — but I am curious about the arrangement between Mr. Tuttle and Mr. Whitfield. Do you know very much about it?"

"Of course. Mr. Tuttle tells me everything. I know all about it."

"Well, would you mind if I ask you, I mean, would you have time to explain it to me?"

"Why are you interested, Janet? Do you expect to inherit Mr. Whitfield's interest?"

"Why, uh, that is a possibility, I suppose, but mainly I'm just curious. And you know, when I asked Mr. Whitfield, he just told me not to worry about it."

"Well, I'm glad Mr. Tuttle's not like that. He wants me to know everything."

"Is their partnership completely dissolved now?"

"Well, yes and no. Janet, I'm working on a quilt and I have to get back home. If you can come over to the house, I'll try to explain it all to you."

"Can I come this evening? I think we'll close the store before dark."

"Well, yes, if you want to."

While Woodbine sorted the mail, Janet cut open the bundle of newspapers and scanned pages. "Oh my," she said aloud.

"Something wrong?" Woodbine asked.

"Yes. Terribly wrong." She finished reading the DEATHS column. "Do you remember the man who came in here looking for Chester Tuttle? Lowell Pretts was his name. He sold his team and wagon and took his sick wife to Denver."

"Yeah, I remember. Why?"

"His wife died yesterday in the Receiving Hospital."

"Aw. Too bad."

Putting the newspaper down, Janet wondered if

172

James Waggoner had found Lowell Pretts, and if so what he had learned.

Just before dark, Janet walked to the east edge of town, crossed the Apache Creek bridge, and knocked on the door of the Tuttle residence. For the second time she was seated in the formal but uncomfortable drawing room. Mrs. Tuttle sat primly in a straight-backed chair across the room, hands in her lap, ankles crossed.

After the pleasantries were over, Janet said, "Let me tell you what I've learned, Mrs. Tuttle, and see if you can add anything."

The older woman waited without speaking.

"Now, as I understand it, I did hear my stepfather say once that he was cattle-rich but land-poor and Mr. Tuttle was land-rich but cattle-poor. I gather that is why they formed a partnership. Then, last fall, right after the railroad reached Denver, Ray Whitfield and his crew gathered four hundred and ten head of prime beeves, including twenty-five of mine, trailed them to Denver, and sold them. He used the proceeds to buy land from Mr. Tuttle."

"That is correct. Only, Mr. Whitfield didn't raise enough money and signed a note for two thousand dollars. Mr. Tuttle holds a mortgage on the Bar W ranch."

"I see. Then my stepfather now owns all the land that Mr. Tuttle had bought from the United States government."

"Except for that mortgage. Well, no, not all. Mr. Tuttle kept title to one hundred acres surrounding the town. He founded Apache Wells, you know."

"I know. The railroad travels almost due west through Apache County, and this spot right here is the only place it comes close to Apache Creek, which runs from the northwest to the southeast. This spot was needed by the railroad as a source of water for the steam engines."

"Yes. Mr. Tuttle was always looking to the future. He gambled that the railroad would come here, and he

173

purchased the land from the U.S. government as soon as it was available for purchase."

"I see. He, as my stepfather said, gambled all his money on land, and had nothing left to buy cattle."

"True. But it was a successful gamble. He and Mr. Whitfield sold beef to the railroad work crews, and later Mr. Tuttle platted the town and sold lots, and now he has sold nearly all of his grazing land. He has earned enough money that he can devote his time to serving the people."

"That's very admirable, Mrs. Tuttle. He not only earned money for himself, his foresight has helped my stepfather to earn enough profit to build a fine house and outbuildings and acquire more land."

"Mr. Whitfield should be grateful to Mr. Tuttle."

"I'm sure he is. Uh, Mrs. Tuttle, do you remember a Lowell Pretts? He was the main witness at the Waggoner brothers' trial, you might recall."

Immediately, the older woman's mouth clamped shut.

Janet said, "He was here, you know, just a few days ago, and—"

Mrs. Tuttle spat out, "Yes, I know."

"Of course you would know. He came here asking for Mr. Tuttle. I just thought his presence might have reminded you of something you had forgotten."

"I told you, Janet, I know no more about that business than anyone else. I was put in charge of keeping the Waggoner boy from running away. I do remember that Mr. Tuttle felt terrible about the whole thing." She stood. "I don't want to be inhospitable, Janet, but I'm expecting Mr. Tuttle home in a day or two, and I have work to do."

Janet stood too. "I apologize for asking so many questions, and I do appreciate your talking to me."

It was dark when she walked to her rented cabin, but she had no fear of the dark. As she walked, she pondered what she had learned that evening. What she had learned wasn't anything that she hadn't already guessed, but now she no longer had to guess.

Chester Tuttle had been raised in some Delaware city near the District of Columbia, and had gone to an eastern university. He had spent a lot of time in the halls of the U.S. Congress and had even worked as an aide to several congressmen. He probably knew what the government was going to do about the problems "out west" before the people "out west" knew. He'd known, for instance, that the government was going to dicker with the Indians and persuade them to cede most of their land east of the Rocky Mountains. He'd been sure, or at least reasonably sure, that the Congress and President Buchanan were going to give the land territorial status. He'd known that when the War Between the States ended, more people would move west and demand land, and the government would then survey the land and offer it for homesteading and for sale. Men already settled on the land would have preemption rights. And what was more important, he'd had reason to believe the Kansas Pacific would eventually lay rails to Denver. The Congress would grant land to the railroad to help pay construction costs, but that wouldn't happen for a few years. In the meantime a man who could grab a huge parcel of that land could raise cattle, deal with the railroad on his own terms when the time came, and even plat a new town.

Yes, Chester Tuttle was the kind of man who looked to the future. But he'd had a lot of luck. And he'd had a lot of help.

Next day, Janet's boss sent her on an errand.

"You know where the Browncrofts live, don't you, Janet, about six miles northwest on the creek?"

"Yes, I think I know."

"You can't get lost. Just follow the creek road. One of the boys rode in this morning with a grocery list. Mrs. Browncroft is feeling too poorly to come to town. I'd go, but I'm buried in paperwork. I'll get the team and

175

wagon. You can handle a team, can't you? They're plumb gentle."

"Of course." She had learned to harness and drive a team of horses the first year she lived on the Whitfield ranch. Woodbine's bay horses were light for a harness team, but the wagon they pulled was light too, with a spring seat. It was just big enough to haul supplies from the railroad depot.

Shortly after noon, wearing a sun bonnet, she climbed to the seat, gathered the driving lines, and chirruped to the team. It was a warm day, but not too hot, and she enjoyed being out of the store and out of town. Her only regret was, she wouldn't be there when the eastbound came through. She hoped James Waggoner would be on it. She had nothing new to tell him, but she hoped he would have something interesting to tell her.

Chapter Thirty

He was disappointed when he learned she was gone. She wouldn't be back until just before dark, he was told. He paid Butler for keeping his roan horse, saddled up, and rode east, following the creek. With nothing else to do, he stopped at The Tree, dismounted, and walked among the weeds and sunflowers, looking for the graves. At first he found no sign of them, but after bending low and parting weeds with his hands, he found a slight depression in the ground near the big cottonwood. It was about six feet long and six feet wide. It had to be a grave. When he failed to find another depression he concluded that his father and uncle were buried in one grave. Side by side.

Bareheaded, he stood there somberly, remembering his father and his uncle Tobe and silently vowing that he would somehow prove them innocent. Finally, he put his hat on and decided he would put the monument at the head of the grave. Which end was the head? He'd have to find out. Horseback again, he rode on up the creek to the dugout. Again he removed his hat and stood over his mother's grave.

Now that he knew for sure that he was marked for death, he was afraid to go inside the dugout again. If Whitfield and his hired man Case happened along he would be trapped inside. Sitting his horse near the entrance, he remembered his dad and uncle talking once about how it would be impossible to escape an Indian attack in there. They'd considered digging a tunnel for an escape route, but never had gotten around to it. It wouldn't have saved his mother anyway. She'd been caught outside the dugout, washing clothes in the creek. The men and her son had been too far away to know what was happening.

In Ma Baker's cafe that evening, he drew the usual stares. He considered asking the waiter who Ma Baker was, but didn't. She was probably back in the kitchen doing the cooking. He wondered if the old man who waited on customers was her husband. His meal over, he thought about going to Janet Carbaugh's cabin. But naw, it was nearly dark, and it wouldn't do to knock on a young lady's door at night without being invited. He'd have to wait until morning. He rode out of town, planning to sleep on the prairie again. About a mile west, he hobbled his horse in a shallow draw, lay fully dressed on his blankets, and tried to work out a plan of action. He had to see Janet Carbaugh before he did anything else. Maybe she had learned more about what happened eleven years ago, and if not, maybe she had an idea what to do next. Would she be willing to question Mrs. Tuttle for him? Anyway, he wanted to talk to her. Dammit, he had to talk to someone.

Pulling off his boots, he tried to sleep. Couldn't. After lying awake for hours he pulled his boots on and stood. It was a warm night with a slight wind coming from the west. In the pale light of a half moon, he could see his hobbled horse grazing and hop-stepping to get at more grass. She would be sleeping now. Restless, he shifted his gunbelt to a comfortable position and walked aimlessly toward town. Apache Wells was dark. No lamplight shone through the windows. A dog barked. Another dog joined in.

Feeling like a prowler in the night, he started to turn back to the open prairie, then realized he was close to her cabin. It too was dark. Everyone in town was asleep. He ought to be asleep. For a long moment he stood there, wishing she would come out and join him in the darkness and knowing that wasn't about to happen. Go on back to your horse and blankets, James Waggoner, he told himself. In the morning he could find her in the mercantile. Yeah, quit this prowling in the dark and get some shut-eye.

Wait. Was that a light in her window? Yeah, a dim light. What was she doing up in the middle of the night? Oh-oh. The cabin door opened and two figures came out. She wasn't one of them. They were too tall and they weren't wearing dresses. What were they wearing? Long underwear? Sure as hell, they were wearing long-handles. And no hats. Jim watched them disappear in the dark behind the cabin. What the humped-up hell?

Uh-oh. For two seconds, Jim stared, unbelieving, fear rising in his chest. Then he started running, running as hard as he could go. The light in the window was brighter. It was flickering.

Come on, feet. Move, feet.

He ran, stumbled over something in the dark, jumped up, and ran. He hit the cabin door with his left shoulder, and didn't even feel the pull of the stitches in his left side. The door crashed open.

She was lying on the floor in the small alcove she used as a bedroom. Flames were climbing the walls, had already surrounded the table, were reaching for the bed. Crackling, popping, spreading fast.

"Janet," he yelled. There was no response. He yanked a blanket off the bed and rolled her in it, covered her from the top of her head to her feet. Her body was limp. The cabin was full of smoke now, and he choked, coughed, gagged. Fire was dancing wildly between him and the door. This was what hell had to be like. Fire, smoke, and heat. The heat was cooking them. Only one thing to do. He picked her up in his arms, mindless of the wound in his side, ducked his head, and ran

179

through the flames for the door.

Stumbling again, he fell onto the floor and lost his hold on her. The air close to the floor was sweet, and he gulped in a lungful. Then, he got her in his arms, jumped up, and ran. He collided with the door frame, bounced off it, ducked his head, and rammed his body forward.

Outside, he fell again, coughing, strangling. His shirttail was burning, and he ripped his shirt apart getting it off. She was still wrapped in the blanket. It didn't appear to be on fire, but he unwrapped her anyway, just to be sure she wasn't burned. She was wearing only a thin nightdress.

On his hands and knees, coughing, bare-chested, he covered her with the blanket again, and gasped, "Janet."

He thought she was dead. Squatting, he coughed, gasped, and strangled until finally he could breath normally. "Janet," he said quietly. "Come on, Janet, live." He'd never begged in his life, but he begged now. "Please, Janet, live."

Her eyes opened.

At first she saw nothing, then her eyes opened wider and she sat up and screamed, "No. Please, no."

"Janet, Janet, it's me. Jim Waggoner. They're gone. Whoever they are, they're gone now."

"James . . ." And she went into coughing convulsions. He sat on the ground beside her, waiting for the coughing to pass. Flames were shooting up through the roof of the cabin now. The heat was hell-hot. Again, he picked her up in his arms and carried her a safe distance away.

"James." The coughing had finally subsided. She spoke in a strangled voice, "James, where did you . . . There were two men. They broke in while I was in bed." Flames threw flickering light across her face.

A shout, and a man came running up, buttoning his suspenders. "Hey. What?" He stopped beside them. "Is there anybody in there?"

"No," Jim said. "There's nobody else."

"Well, what . . . ?"

A woman joined him, her gray hair down to her shoulders, a faded plaid robe wrapped around a long nightdress. "It's Janet Carbaugh. Janet, are you hurt?"

"No, I don't think so." She rubbed her right temple. "A sore spot, that's all."

"How did it happen? A lamp fall over?"

"No, I . . ." She picked herself up and stood, holding the blanket tight around her shoulders. "I'll have to report this to the sheriff. Someone hit me on the head and set fire to my cabin."

"What? Who would do that?"

"Are you sure, Janet?"

Another man ran up, and another. Soon a half-dozen men and four women had gathered, but they could do nothing more than watch the cabin roof fall in and the walls collapse.

A plump woman with brown hair sticking out in all directions was looking from Janet to Jim. "What was you doin'? You in your bedclothes and him with no shirt."

Janet turned on her. "Now, just a gosh-darned minute. He saved my life. I don't know where he came from or how he happened to be here, but he saved my life."

"Two men, you say?"

"Yes. They broke in while I was asleep."

"Here comes the sheriff."

The crowd gathered to hear every word as Janet told the lawman what had happened. "This sounds strange, I know," she said, "but they were wearing only their underwear. Long underwear. They had bandannas over their heads and faces."

"Uh-huh." The woman with wild hair was disbelieving. "Sure."

Sheriff Rogers gave the woman a hard look, then

181

turned back to Janet. "You don't know who they were, then, or why they wanted to kill you?"

"No, I . . ." When she thought about it she knew why, but she didn't want to explain it to everyone. "I don't know."

Now the sheriff was looking at Jim. Jim felt indecent without a shirt. "Seems like you draw trouble like a lamp draws a moth. What were you doing here?"

Janet answered, "That's nobody's business. He can come and go as he pleases."

"Uh-huh," said the wild-haired woman. "Sure."

"Listen," Jim said, hands on hips, "I saw them too. Two men in long johns."

"Now, why would any man want to go around like that?" The answer occurred to him, and he added, "Well, if they meant to kill Miss Carbaugh, why would they care if she recognized them by their clothes?"

"There is always a chance that somebody else saw them," Jim argued.

Another woman said, "He's that Waggoner boy, ain't he? Ever'body knows she's sweet on him."

"Now listen." Janet's brown eyes flashed in the firelight. Then she shrugged. "Aw, what's the use. You wouldn't understand."

"Well, anyway," the sheriff put in, "nobody was hurt, and I'm mighty glad of that. What you do, Miss Carbaugh is no business of mine." Turning to the crowd, he said, "There's nothing to be done now. The house is gone and so is everything in it."

Still another woman stepped out of the crowd, a slender woman with black hair and age wrinkles around her eyes and throat. "Janet, why don't you come home with me. Lord knows I've got plenty of room, and I think my clothes will fit you."

"Thank you, Mrs. Jamison." To Jim she said, "I have to talk with you, Jim. It's important. Come and see me today, will you?"

"Sure, Miss Carbaugh. I need to talk to you too."

Only a pile of hot ashes with burning red streaks through it remained of the cabin. The stove and lengths of stovepipe were all that was left of the interior. "Wal, I don't reckon she's a-goin' to spread," a man said.

"Naw, she's about to burn herself out."

"Might as well go back to bed."

For a while, Jim stood there alone. Shirtless, he shivered in the late-night chill. Then, head down, he started walking back to the open prairie and his horse and blankets. Rage was boiling within him. He felt like yelling, cursing to the sky. Instead he muttered, "They tried to get rid of me and now they've tried to get rid of her. This has got to come to an end. I've got to stop them.

"Even if I have to kill them."

Chapter Thirty-one

Mrs. Jamison's dress dragged on the floor when Janet put it on, and though they pinned up the hem it looked and felt awkward. She had no choice but to wear it to the store. Woodbine was talkative. "Why in the world would anyone want to burn down your house with you in it, Janet? Does this have anything to do with young Waggoner? Why don't you stay away from him? He's caused trouble ever since he came here."

"It's not his fault. He didn't cause trouble. Others have caused trouble."

Woodbine offered to sell her a dress on credit. She chose instead a boy's duck pants, shirt, and shoes. "I'll have to pay you out of my wages," she said. "My money—all I had saved—burned with the house."

"Your credit is good anytime. And yes, I can manage without you here today. Are you going back to the ranch to live now?"

"No. Only to get some clothes."

"Janet." Woodbine was worried. "I can't imagine why anyone would want to harm you, but they might try again, you know. What are you going to do?"

"Why, I'll just have to be careful."

"I'll . . . if you want to stay at the ranch and away from town, I'll manage without you somehow. I don't know who I can hire to replace you, but I can hire someone. I'll have to hire another clerk anyway when you go back to school."

"When the time comes I'll help you find someone, but don't . . ." A wane smile turned up the corners of her mouth briefly. "Don't replace me just yet."

"All right, Janet."

She rode out of town sitting astraddle a man's saddle. As she crossed the bridge, she enjoyed hearing the horse's hooves *cloppity-clopping* on the planks. She rode past the Tuttle house and on southeast along the creek. Her eyes were moving constantly, watching for anything human. Before she topped a low hill, she reined up, studied her surroundings, and approached the crest of the hill cautiously, ready to wheel the horse around and ride back to town at a gallop. But she saw no one. She would be safe when she got to the ranch house, she believed. Her stepfather wouldn't harm her, and Poco and most of the crew were not her enemies. In fact, she thought with a grim smile, if anyone tried to harm her at the Bar W they'd have two-thirds of the crew on their necks. The house and outbuildings were a welcome sight.

But the only man there was Poco.

"Ray and the boys rode out at daylight," he said. "I don't look for them back till late."

Poco had on a clean apron now and a shirt with the sleeves rolled up. And, Janet discovered when she looked around, the house had been straightened inside. No clothes, boots, or scraps of leather littered the living room. Dust was thick everywhere, and the rug needed cleaning, but everything was in its place.

"What has happened in here?" she asked.

"Aw, the boss got mad and said he was through livin' like a pack rat, and started muckin' the place out."

"Did he tell you to put on a shirt?"

"Wal, he sorta hinted at it."

Janet had to smile at that. She climbed the stairs to her room and changed out of the boy's clothes. The blue cotton dress she chose was full enough in the skirt that it would fit the seat of a saddle and allow her to ride astraddle. Back in the kitchen, she accepted Poco's offer of a cup of coffee. Sitting at the kitchen table, she said, "Tell me something, Poco, do you know if anyone from here was in town late last night?"

"I don't know. I sleep on the back porch, and I don't know who goes in or out of the bunkhouse. I used ta sleep in the bunkhouse, but I get up too early, and some a the boys griped, said I make too much noise."

"Oh, I see. Well, were there any horses left in the corral last night that some of the men could have ridden to town?"

"Don't think so. Just one night horse. Yeah, I remember, old Abe had to jangle the remuda this mornin', and he had to do it by hisself 'cuz there was only one horse."

Janet pondered that. Apache Wells was only about four miles away — walking distance, but cowboys didn't like to walk. The two men who'd hit her on the head and set fire to her rented house hadn't come from here. Unless . . .

"Do Case and Job still work here?"

"Case don't. The boss fired 'im. Day before yestiday. Sent 'im down the road a-talkin' to hisself."

Astounded, Janet said, "He did?"

"Yep."

"Any particular reason?"

"Waren't none a my business. But that Case is a mean, uh, one. He's mean to hosses and he's mean to men."

"How about Job? He and Case seemed to be pretty thick."

"He's still here. Least he was this mornin'. Tell you the truth, I don't think he was all that thick with Case. He just done like he was told."

"Oh, I see. But Case could have been in town last night?"

"Yep. 'Less he quit the country. He had his own hoss."

"Hmm. Well, I have to see Ray as soon as possible, and I guess the soonest way is to wait here for him."

"I'll fix you some chuck anytime you want it, Miss

Janet."

"Thanks, Poco." She didn't tell him about the fire.

For the second time in two days Jim went to the Apache Wells Mercantile to see Janet only to learn that she wasn't there. And this time, her boss, Woodbine, wouldn't tell him where she was.

"After what happened last night, I don't think she wants anyone to know her whereabouts," he said.

"Well, uh . . ." Jim didn't know what to say to that. "Well, would you tell me, is she coming back?"

"Yeah, she'll be back."

"She said she wanted to see me today, and I need to see her."

"Listen, son." Woodbine leaned on the long counter with his arms crossed on top of it. "I . . . we all know how you feel. I'd feel the same way, I think. But what happened way back in 1860 is over. Nothing can be done about it now. Most folks who are here now had nothing to do with it. And since you came here there've been shots fired and a house burned down. Two men tried to kill Janet because of you. Why don't you just get on your horse and ride on?"

Jim had to think about it before he spoke again. "You're right. She's in danger because of me — because she got in the middle of my troubles. But, dammit, somebody tried to kill her last night, and they had a reason. I know why and she knows why, and they might try again."

"I told her that. She promised she'd be careful. That was all I could do."

All Jim could do then was look down, turn around, and walk out.

He went to Mrs. Jamison's house, knocked on the door, and waited. When the black-haired woman opened the door, he apologized, and said it was important that he find Janet.

Mrs. Jamison's mouth was pinched at first, then she

relaxed. "Well, seeing as how it was you that saved her last night, I'd tell you if I knew, but I don't know."

"Well, thanks anyway." Jim stepped off the porch, untied his roan horse at a hitchrail, and walked, head down, leading the horse.

He hated the idea of just sitting somewhere waiting for her to come back. He had to do something but he didn't know what to do. If he knew who'd tried to burn Janet alive last night, he'd hunt them down and pump bullets into them. But he didn't know. Or, he could ride to Denver, hunt up Chester Tuttle, and pump a couple of .44 balls into him. Tuttle was behind the whole thing. He and Raymond Whitfield. Whitfield had something to do with it all. With them dead, Janet would be safe and Apache Wells would be a quiet peaceful town again.

Of course, Jim would be a hunted man for the rest of his life. The lawdogs wouldn't let the two murders go unavenged. Especially if one of the deceased was an important public bigshot like Chester Tuttle. Only Jim knew what kind of man the politician really was. Janet knew he had pulled some kind of scheme eleven years ago, but she didn't know about his other wife. If Tuttle was killed, the truth about him would come out eventually, but Jim would still be charged with murder.

All right, so he'd be a wanted man. Maybe it would be worth it. Janet would be safe, and he'd have his revenge. There was a lot of country in the western territories. A man could make himself hard to find. Maybe that's what he ought to do. But he sure would like to see Janet first.

He walked his horse to Butler's barn. If he had to wait, the horse might as well be fed some hay instead of being tied to a hitchrail or hobbled on the prairie. Who knows, he might have to leave town in a hurry, and he might need a well-fed, well-rested horse. At Butler's he unsaddled and turned the horse into a feed lot where a dozen others were eating out of a wooden hay rack. Butler demanded to be paid in advance, so Jim paid him.

He was walking out of the barn, trying to decide where

to wait, when he saw two men coming toward him. He recognized one immediately. Case. And then the other. No. Couldn't be. It was the dandy who'd wanted to kill him in a Denver saloon, the one with the pearl-handled pistol in a shoulder holster. How did he get here? On the same train with Jim? Sure. There was no other way. He'd changed to a workingman's clothes, and managed to ride the same train without Jim seeing him.

He'd been sent here. Jim knew why.

They were the two who'd tried to kill Janet. Jim had silently vowed to stop them. Right now and right here was a good place to stop them permanently.

Chapter Thirty-two

They saw Jim at the same time he saw them. They stopped a moment, and Case said something in a low voice to the other man. Then they separated, walking toward Jim.

Jim knew what they were doing. They were getting on either side of him where he would be caught between them. He knew he ought to draw the Colt and shoot right now. Shoot them down, his mind said. Don't let them shoot first. His hand hovered over the Colt, but he didn't draw it. He couldn't just start shooting and killing without a warning of some kind.

He barked, "Hold it right there."

They stopped. Case's hand was close to the sixgun on his hip, and the dandy's hand was near the shoulder holster.

"Take one more step and I'll shoot you, Case, and then I'll shoot your partner."

"You're just itchin' for a fight, ain't you, kid."

"Yeah. After what happened last night I want you two long gone."

"What if we ain't ready to leave?"

Jim considered that. He had to shoot or let them shoot him. This was what old Zack Dawson had called a Dead Man's Showdown. "All right." He was surprised at how calm he was. "I'm going to give you a chance. There are two of you. Draw your guns and start blasting."

190

He was expecting it. He was ready. Case was the most dangerous. He'd try to outdraw and outshoot Case, then turn half around and shoot the dandy. He'd have to draw and shoot as fast as he ever had. This wasn't for practice. Someone was going to die.

Long seconds went by. No one moved. Someone had to move first. Jim's nerves were beginning to tighten. A knot was forming in his stomach. He couldn't stay calm much longer. He had to draw and shoot now.

"Hey." The quiet was broken. "Hey, hold on there." Sheriff Rogers came up on the run. "What the hell's going on here? You men. Get your hands away from those guns. Don't move."

Jim was afraid to take his eyes off Case's gunhand — until the sheriff got between them, his own gun drawn. "What the hell's going on here?" the sheriff demanded.

It was Butler who answered, "They was just mindin' their own business when this kid braced 'em."

"Is that right, Waggoner?" Sheriff Rogers turned his gun Jim's way.

"I don't know who braced who, but these sons of bitches tried to kill Janet Carbaugh last night, and they know I know it."

Case said, "That's a goddamn lie. He's a goddamn liar."

"You got any proof of that, Waggoner?"

Jim hooked his thumbs in his gunbelt and admitted, "No."

"Then how in hell can you accuse them of it?"

"They did it. That one" — Jim pointed to the dandy — "tried to kill me in Denver. Somebody sent him here to finish the job and to kill Miss Carbaugh."

"Huh," the dandy snorted, "I never saw this punkin roller before in my life."

"He's good at makin' up stories," Case said. "He's a goddamn liar."

Jim's face was hot, and rage made his voice tremble. "You're the liar. You lied about a lot of things. You stole my money and lied about that. You tried to kill me in the dark and said I was trying to steal a horse. That was another lie. Now you're lying again."

"I don't know who's lying," the sheriff said, "but I ought to lock up the whole damned bunch of you. I'm telling you right now, all of you, if there's any shooting, I'll know who to look for and some damned body is going to wish he'd never been born. Now . . ." he looked from one man to another. "I want all three of you to get your sorry asses out of my county. If I see any of you here after today, I'm going to throw your sorry asses in the hoosegow and keep you there till you ain't nothing but a puddle of water. Get it?"

No one spoke, and the sheriff yelled, "Get it?"

Jim looked down. He didn't want to leave without seeing Janet, but if he had to leave, he knew what he'd do. He'd watch for a chance and shoot Raymond Whitfield, then go to Denver and shoot Chester Tuttle. He'd be branded a killer. But there was nothing else to do.

"Goddamn it, Waggoner, do you understand what I said?"

"Yeah," Jim answered, looking down. He wanted no fight with Sheriff Rogers.

"How about you, Case? And you, whatever the hell your name is?"

"We was leavin' anyways," Case answered.

"I'm waiting to see Miss Carbaugh," Jim said. "She ought to be back pretty soon."

"Case? Go get your wages from Ray Whitfield and ride."

"I done quit," Case said.

"Then get on your horses and ride now."

Janet was relieved when she looked out a window of the big house and saw riders coming. One of them was her stepfather. Instead of waiting for him to unsaddle his horse and come to the house, she went out to the corrals to meet him.

"Janet." Ray Whitfield smiled. "What brings you out

192

here?"

"I have to talk to you, Ray. Can we go to the house?"

"Sure, Janet. Soon's I turn this horse out."

"Better keep a horse up, Ray. You might have to go to town."

His bushy eyebrows came together as he studied her face. "Something wrong? Something happen?" Three cowboys were watching, listening. Janet didn't answer, but turned and walked back to the house. Within a few minutes, Whitfield came in through the kitchen door.

"What happened, Janet?"

She told him about two men who had broken into her rented house while she was asleep, hit her on the head, and set fire to the house. She told him how James Waggoner had carried her out.

A shadow passed over the rancher's face. His jaw muscles bulged. Then he said, "Are you hurt, Janet?"

"No."

He turned his head away and looked blankly out the window. He muttered, "Those sons of bitches."

"What?" Janet was surprised by his language. "Who?"

"I think I know who." He continued staring out the window, not speaking. Then, "Did you say you talked to this Lowell Pretts?"

"Yes, I did."

"Then I know who."

"Who, Ray?"

For a long moment, he was silent. "Who?" Janet asked again.

"Did you see Case in town?"

"No. Poco said you fired him."

"That I did. Should have fired him long ago."

"I've often wondered why you kept him around. I got the impression some time ago that you didn't like him."

Whitfield turned to her, his face still cold. "Did you know, Janet, that Chester Tuttle holds a note on this land? A two-thousand-dollar note?"

"I, uh, yes, I knew that."

"Chet thinks because he holds a note on this outfit he ought to tell me how to run it. He hired Case. Now I know why."

"Why?"

No answer came from the cattleman. He turned his head away and resumed staring at the window. Finally, he spun on his heels and left the room. "Wait here."

Janet waited. When Whitfield came back, he was buttoning a shirt pocket. "Can you ride a horse in that outfit?"

"Yes. Why?"

"We're going to town. I've got something to say to the sheriff, and I'll put it in writing."

"What, Ray? What is it?"

"Come on."

She had to run to keep up with him as he walked to the corrals. The prairie sun hung low in the western sky, but hadn't yet touched the horizon. At the corrals Whitfield caught a fresh horse and saddled it. She tightened the cinches on her horse, climbed into the saddle, and arranged her long skirt so it covered her legs down to her ankles.

"Did you say we're going to see Sheriff Rogers?"

Still he didn't answer. They rode for a half-mile at a steady trot before he spoke again, muttering through his teeth, "They think they can get by with anything. Well, by God, when they try to kill my daughter they're going too damn far. Way too far."

She wanted to know who, but she realized it was useless to ask.

Whitfield continued muttering. "Yes, by God, they've done gone and dirtied the nest. What kind of man do they think I am? Do they think I'll let 'em get by with this?" He rode silently a moment. "It's time to end the whole damned shooting match."

She couldn't help it, she had to ask, "For heaven's sake, Ray, who?"

Turning his head her way, he said, "Take a good look at

me, Janet, 'cause after I tell my story to the sheriff, you won't want to see me again."

"Why, Ray?"

No answer. Suddenly, the rancher reined up. "Goddamn."

Looking in the direction he was looking, she saw them.

"Goddamn," he muttered again. "They're coming. Four of them."

Squinting, she said, "That's Case, isn't it? Who are the others."

"They ain't friends. They're after our hides, Janet. Let's ride."

Chapter Thirty-three

The closer to the horizon the sun moved, the more Jim Waggoner worried. She should have been back by now. Something had happened to her. The two jaspers who'd tried to kill her had caught her away from town somewhere. He saddled his roan horse, but didn't mount. Could she have come back to town without his seeing her? He'd been keeping an eye on the Apache Wells Mercantile, and he believed she hadn't returned there. Walking, leading the horse, he went to Mrs. Jamison's and again knocked on the door. There was no answer. Mrs. Jamison had gone to the mercantile, or to a neighbor's to visit.

Damn.

Mounted now, he rode to the store, got down, and tied the horse to a hitchrail. No, Woodbine said, Miss Carbaugh hadn't returned. No, he believed she would not want her whereabouts known. Outside, Jim mounted the horse again and rode to Butler's barn. Butler was cleaning a wooden water tank with a stiff brush and a bucket of water. He was no help.

"How in hell would I know where she went? She got on her horse and went, that's all I know. It's gonna be sundown pretty soon. You better haul your ass out of here your ownself. Tom Rogers don't get mad very much, but he's mad now."

"I'm not leaving till I'm sure Miss Carbaugh is safe,

aw or no law. Didn't you even see which way she went?"

"East. She rode east."

"Any idea where?"

"Yeah, I got an idea where, but it ain't none of your business."

"Why? Why won't you tell me? What did I ever do to you?"

"You ain't done nothin' to me and you ain't a-goin' to, either. I happen to be a friend of Case's and Ray Whitfield's, and if they don't like you, I don't like you."

Jim remembered seeing Butler in the Prairie Rose saloon the day he'd gotten his money back at gunpoint, and he remembered Butler being in the barn when he'd punched Whitfield. "You ain't particular about your friends, are you?" He went back to his horse and mounted.

East. What was east of town that would interest Janet Carbaugh? Let's see, Chester Tuttle's house was on the east side, across the bridge. Is she visiting with Mrs. Tuttle? Not likely. If that was her destination she would have walked. There was The Tree, and about a mile beyond that was the old Waggoner dugout. Another couple of miles east, or southeast, was the Whitfield ranch house.

The sun would soon touch the western horizon now. It wasn't long until dark. If she didn't show up by dark, he'd be sick with worry. What to do? Well, the Tuttle house was near. It would be a waste of time to go there, but he could think of nothing else to do. He rode across the bridge. The roan horse still wasn't used to hearing its own hoofbeats on the planks, and it walked with short, quick steps, ready to bolt. On the other side, Jim turned the horse up the short, rutted private road to the Tuttle house. When he knocked on the door he was surprised.

It was Chester Tuttle who opened the door.

Both men were surprised. Tuttle was wearing a white

shirt, but no coat and no tie. His jaw dropped open, and his mouth moved without speaking. Jim instinctively stepped back a step and his right hand went to the butt of the Colt.

The politician eyed the gun and half-closed the door, ready to slam it. "What do you want?"

Forcing himself to relax, Jim hooked his thumbs inside the gunbelt. "I came here looking for Janet Carbaugh. Your wife seems to be friendly with her."

"Why didn't you stay in Denver?"

"I'm still looking for answers, and I'm betting the answers are right here."

"I think you know all there is to know about what happened at that trial."

"I don't think so. And neither does Miss Carbaugh. She's looking for answers too. That's why somebody tried to kill her last night."

"I heard about that. What's that got to do with me?"

Jim didn't want to answer that question, and he repeated, "I'm looking for Miss Carbaugh. I thought she might be here."

A woman's voice came from inside the house, "Who is it, Chester?"

"It's that Waggoner boy. He's looking for Janet Carbaugh."

Mrs. Tuttle came forward, but her husband blocked the door and she had to speak from behind him. "I haven't seen her. I heard about the fire last night, and I heard it was you who saved her. Did she disappear?"

"I've been told she got on a horse at Butler's barn and rode east. Have you any idea, Mrs. Tuttle, where she went?"

Chester Tuttle interrupted, "We don't know where she went, and after what you accused me of in Denver, you are not welcome at my house. Good evening." He closed the door.

"Aw, for crying out loud," Jim muttered to himself as he walked off the porch.

198

The four riders had split, with two angling behind Janet and Raymond Whitfield while the other two stayed on the wagon road. It was obvious now that they didn't intend to let the rancher and his stepdaughter get to town. Janet and Whitfield booted their horses into a run, cutting across a long curve in the road, trying to get around the two and beat them to the creek crossing and Apache Wells. But the riders had the angle on them and were about to head them off. Whitfield was spurring recklessly. Janet was whipping her horse with the ends of the bridle reins. Both horses were running as hard as they could go, dodging sagebrush, jumping gulleys.

A shot. At the same instant a bullet whistled dangerously close. When the next shot came, Janet screamed, "They're trying to kill us."

Whitfield yelled, "Ride, Janet. Ride like hell."

"We can't make it. We can't beat them."

Bringing his mount to a sliding stop, Whitfield yelled, "Hold up. You're right. Let's head back to the ranch." He waited until Janet had her horse stopped and turned back, then cursed. "Goddamn it, two of 'em are cutting us off there too. "Goddamn it." He started to dismount. "I can shoot better on foot. I'll try to slow 'em down, Janet. Ride for the house."

"No," she yelled. "It's hopeless. There's the dugout. Let's ride for the dugout."

"What dugout?"

"The old Waggoner dugout."

"Oh. Yeah. Come on." He spurred his horse into a dead run again. "Ride, Janet. Goose that pony." She was soon beside him, the wind whipping her hair, whipping her long dress. Both horses were running flat out.

There was another shot, and another. Even with the wind in her ears, Janet heard a bullet whine past her head. She whipped her horse with the bridle reins. "Come on, fella, come on, please." The horse was doing its best.

Jim rode east at a slow walk, trying to pick up her trail. There were too many horse tracks on the wagon road near town, and he had no way of knowing which tracks were left by her horse. He reined up several times to study the ground, hoping for some kind of sign. Surely she had stayed on the road. Where else would she go? And why go east? Why go anywhere, for that matter? Why wouldn't that goddamn knothead Woodbine tell him where she'd gone? The sun was sinking. It would be dark in a another hour. Nothing to do but keep looking and hoping to cut her sign, find some kind of clue.

He meant it when he'd told Butler he wasn't leaving Apache County until he knew she was safe. Or knew what happened to her. He wanted no fight with a lawman, but, by God, he wasn't going to be run off just yet, either. And if anything happened to Janet, some damn body was going to bleed. Tuttle. Son of a bitch must have come in on the eastbound. Decided to pay his wife a visit, had he? What would Mrs. Tuttle do if she knew about the redheaded wife in Denver? Would she leave him? Well, what happened between Tuttle and his wife was none of Jim's business. What was his business now was Janet and her safety.

Goddamn town anyway. Goddamn people wouldn't even talk to him. Everybody acted like he had the smallpox. Sons of bitches.

Their horses were tiring. The four horses coming at them were tiring too. The four men were shooting, trying to at least hit one of their horses and put them afoot. Sooner or later they would succeed. Janet and

200

Whitfield were riding side by side. Whitfield had switched sides once to put himself between their pursuers and his stepdaughter.

"Not much farther," Janet yelled. She reined her horse to the right. "Over here. Over here under the bluff." A bullet sang an angry song past her left ear.

"I don't think this horse is gonna make it," Whitfield yelled. "If I stop, go on, Janet. Keep going."

Her horse stumbled, regained its balance, and continued running. Janet whipped it with her bridle reins. "I'm sorry. Please don't quit. We're close."

Then they were on top of the cutbank, near Mrs. Waggoner's grave, and the horses were plunging off the cutbank in front of the dugout. Whitfield dismounted on the run, his sixgun in his hand, looking back, ready to shoot. Janet had to bring her horse to a stop, disentangle her long skirt, and slide out of the saddle.

"Get inside," Whitfield barked. "I'll hold 'em off."

She ran inside, scrambled over a pile of dirt that young Waggoner had shoveled out the back end of the dugout, and fell on her face behind it. She jumped up immediately, and when her stepfather started clambering over the pile of dirt, she grabbed his left arm and helped pull him over.

A shot thumped into the back end of the cave and another kicked dirt in Whitfield's face. Instead of ducking his head, he knelt behind the dirt and looked for someone to shoot at. When he saw a man out front, he fired without taking careful aim. The sound of the explosion in the dugout was painful to the ears.

Muttering, Whitfield said, "They, by God, know we're forted up now and can, by God, shoot back."

"They can't get us in here, can they, Ray?"

"Not as long as there's daylight. We can hold 'em off all day."

"But what will we do?"

Shaking his head, Whitfield answered, "I don't know. We're only about a mile and a half from town. Maybe

201

. . . maybe somebody'll hear all the gunfire and come to see what's going on."

"Yes. Maybe somebody will bring the sheriff."

"Maybe," Whitfield grunted. "A hell of a big word."

Chapter Thirty-four

Jim Waggoner was glad he'd brought his saddlebags and all his belongings with him. He, for sure, was going to spend another night on the prairie. He'd decided he'd go back to town after dark and ask Mrs. Jamison if Janet had returned. If she hadn't, he'd camp on the east side someplace. In the morning, he'd go back and ask again. If the damned sheriff didn't like it, they'd just have to fight it out. He had no quarrel with Tom Rogers, but he wasn't going to be pushed too far by the law either. His stomach reminded him that he'd had nothing to eat since early morning. A throbbing in his left side reminded him the stitches were still there. But hunger and pain were not his main problems. Janet. Where was she? She couldn't have gone to the Whitfield ranch house, could she? What in hell would she be doing there? As far as Jim knew, there wasn't another house for miles and miles, but maybe there was a ranch family over east somewhere, a family she was friends with.

Yeah, that's probably where she was. If so, she was safe. But, damn, he wished he knew for sure.

Dark was coming on fast by the time he reached The Tree and the graves. He got down, loosened the cinches, and let the horse graze. When he saw that the horse was cropping grass on the graves, his first impulse was to lead it away. But on second thought, his dad and uncle would probably like having a good horse graze over them. Jim sat cross-legged on the ground.

May they rest in peace.

It was growing dark in the dugout. No shots had been fired for ten minutes or more, but Janet and her stepfather knew the men were out there. Just what they were planning to do was puzzling.

"When it gets dark enough, we might slip out and make ourselves hard to find in the weeds along the creek," Whitfield said. "But at the same time, they might slip in."

Suddenly, he turned to Janet. "Here, take this gun. You've seen us men shoot guns, haven't you? Look, the hammer's already back, so all you have to do is point it and pull the trigger. Keep your eyes open."

She took the big pistol and held it in both hands. Her hands were unsteady. "What are you going to do, Ray?"

"I've got some writing to do, and I have to do it before it gets dark."

"Writing? What kind of writing?"

"If I get a chance to finish it, you'll see." He unbuttoned a shirt pocket and took out two folded sheets of paper and a lead pencil. He knelt at the Waggoners' old wooden table. Face screwed up in thought, he began writing. Janet watched him, curious, then remembered she had to watch the front of the dugout.

It was quiet. At times she heard men talking outside. At times she could hear the lead pencil scraping the paper. She had to glance at her stepfather now and then.

A bullet thudded into the pile of dirt near her face. She pulled her head down. Remembering that she had to keep watch, she peered over the dirt again. She saw no one. Whitfield's scratching continued. With trembling hands, Janet held the pistol on top of the dirt, her finger on the trigger. She tried to stop her hands from trembling.

My God, she thought. I'm scared.

* * *

It was almost dark now. Jim decided to wait another half-hour, then go back to town. No use looking for her in the dark. She was either in town, at some rancher's house or . . . or dead.

And, damn — Jim's heart sunk lower when he remembered — she'd asked him to look her up today. She wanted to talk to him as much as he wanted to talk to her. She hadn't planned to be gone all day.

She was probably dead. And it was because of him. If he hadn't come back to Apache Creek, Janet Carbaugh would be alive and going back to school in Denver this fall and living and . . . Jim gulped . . . marrying and . . .

He felt like cursing himself. For the past eleven years he'd carried the memory of his dad and uncle hanging by their necks. Now this. This was even worse. It seemed he was doomed to carrying bad memories.

Well, by God, he was through trying to forget and forgive. He knew who was responsible for the hangings and he knew who was responsible for Janet's death. He would . . . well, first he'd get the sheriff to organize a posse to hunt for Janet. Or her body. Then he'd just walk up to Chester Tuttle and empty the Colt .44 in his belly. Then?

Maybe he'd run for it. Or maybe he'd just hand his gun over to Sheriff Rogers and wait himself for the hangman's noose.

Either way, Jim couldn't help feeling that his life was over.

"All right," Raymond Whitfield said standing, stretching his legs one at a time. "See anyone out there, Janet?"

"I haven't seen anyone, but they haven't left. I can hear them. Sounds like they're breaking wood."

"Breaking wood?" Whitfield knelt beside her behind the pile of dirt. "You don't suppose they're gonna start a fire and smoke us out."

"Oh, my gosh. What can we do?"

205

"Hope. Just hope the wind blows the wrong way. Be dark in a few minutes. Here." He handed her two sheets of paper. "I wish I didn't have to write this, but I want you to know about this, and you'd better read it before it gets so dark you can't read."

Taking the paper from his hand, she sat on the dirt floor of the dugout. Barely enough light came through the opening to enable her to make out the words.

"Janet." Whitfield's voice was low, sad, painful. "You're gonna hate me." He shook his head. "Read it."

Holding the paper high to get as much light on it as she could, Janet read:

I, Raymond Whitfield, being of sound mind, do hereby make this confeshon. Janet ignored the misspelled word, glanced at her stepfather and read on:

In August of the year eighteen hundred and sixty, two men were hung from the limb of a cottonwood tree on the edge of a creek known as Apache Creek. They were James and Tobe Waggoner. Their bodies are berred near the tree. They are the victims of an unjust trial. I, Raymond Whitfield, and Chester Tuttle claimed a section of land apiece on each side of two sections of land claimed by the Waggoner brothers. We beleeved all the land around there would be very valuable in the future and we wanted the two sections claimed by the Waggoner brothers. In early August a man named Lowell Pretts came to Chester Tuttle's house and said he was the rightful owner of two brindle bulls which was then wearing the Waggoner brother's running w brand.

Glancing at her stepfather, squinting at the paper, Janet read on: *Lowell Pretts said some of his cattle were drove off his place in west Kansas territory in the spring of eighteen hundred and fifty-nine. He said he saw three men drive them off, but lost sight of them when they shot at him. He said he did not recognize the men. He said he was not certain the Waggoner brothers were among the ones that drove his cattle off. When Chester Tuttle told me about it I said we ought to get Lowell Pretts to blame the Waggoner brothers and we could get there land. Chester Tuttle payed Lowell Pretts to say in the Claims Court trial that James and Tobe Waggoner were the guilty ones. I was on the jury that voted to hang James and Tobe*

Waggoner.

Raymond Whitfield.

Janet put the paper down. Tears filled her eyes. "Oh, Ray. How could you do it?"

The rancher was near tears himself. "All I can say, Janet, is I didn't mean for them to be hung. I am a thief and a liar, but I didn't mean for them to be hung. I thought they'd be ordered out of the territory, that's all. I'm not making excuses. I was a party to hanging two innocent men."

"But why didn't you . . . ?"

"I was on the jury, like I said there, and I was outvoted."

Janet spoke through tears, "But you could have told them the truth."

"I could have. I didn't. I am guilty of murder."

"Oh, my God."

"I don't blame you for hating me. I hate myself. A lot of times I felt like going to some lawyer or some government honcho somewhere and telling the truth. I didn't. I am a weak man."

"But," Janet sniffed, "why . . . when the Waggoner boy came back, why did you lock him in jail for something he didn't do?"

"I have to admit I was afraid of him. I'm not proud of it. I thought we could maybe scare him off. But I had nothing to do with shooting at him, and I had nothing to do with stealing the bill of sale for his horse. Case did that. And now that I think of it, I'll bet old Tuttle put him up to it. Somebody sent word to Chester Tuttle about the boy coming back."

Sobbing, Janet wailed, "Oh, Ray."

Her sobbing was cut short by a gunshot. The bullet slammed into the dirt wall behind them. Another bullet plowed a furrow in the top of the dirt pile.

"Duck your head, Janet, they're coming."

She squatted behind the dirt. Whitfield fired a booming shot from his pistol. He said, "They're throwing sticks in front of the cave. They're gonna get a pile of 'em.

They're gonna try to smoke us out."

He looked for a target, but not a man showed himself. Instead, they stood back away from the front of the cave and tossed dry sticks until they had a pile near the door. Then a burning stick was tossed into the pile. More sticks started burning.

But Janet wasn't thinking about the danger they were in. She was thinking about two innocent men hanging from a tree limb and a young boy left homeless. And her stepfather. A murderer.

Chapter Thirty-five

It was dark now, and Jim started tightening the cinches on his saddle. He paused, listening . Was that a gunshot? Where did it come from? Over east? Southeast? Straining his ears, he listened. Yeah, there was another shot. Who the hell was shooting? Did that have anything to do with Janet?

"Well, hell," he said to the horse, "maybe we ought to go and find out. Somebody is shooting at somebody. They sure ain't hunting meat in the dark." He swung into the saddle and turned the horse away from the creek and onto the road. "Wish it wasn't so dark, so I could see what's going on."

Flames filled the wood-framed opening to the dugout. Janet and Raymond Whitfield were in the firelight while the four men outside were in the dark.

"We're in a bad spot, Janet," Whitfield said. "They can see in here but we can't see out there."

"Yes." Her mind was still on the confession she had read. She folded the paper carefully and tried to hand it to her stepfather.

"No, you keep it. In case something happens to me. Give it to the sheriff, or take it to Denver and give it to a judge."

"I don't . . . really . . ." Her mind was numb from what

209

she'd just learned.

"The wind's in our favor now, but it could shift."

"Yes." She put the paper in the pocket of her dress.

"They're throwing more wood on the fire. There's a lot of firewood along the creek."

Her mind still refused to switch to the present, to the danger they were in. "Yes."

Whitfield repeated, "We're in a bad spot."

They were silent a moment. Flames crackled. The interior of the dugout was getting warm. Firelight danced on Whitfield's face, giving him a weird, devilish look. Janet was seeing him as a devil.

"Janet?"

"Yes."

"I know you can't forgive me for what I did. I wish there was something I could do to make up for it."

Sourly, blinking back tears, she said, "There's nothing."

"You're like a daughter to me. Like my real daughter. That's why I went to that judge in Kansas Territory and adopted you legally."

"Yes."

Then a bullet kicked dirt over both of them, and Janet's mind finally registered the danger. She again saw Whitfield as her stepfather the man who had helped raise her.

"I'm begging, Janet. I never begged before. Please try to forgive me."

"I remember," Janet said slowly, thoughtfully, "that you treated my mother and me very well. You were good to me. I'll always remember that, Ray."

"Thank God I did something right."

More silence. Another bullet hit the dirt near Whitfield's face. The flames were climbing higher. The inside of the dugout was getting warmer.

"Here's what we're gonna do, Janet. They know we can't stay in here much longer and they're waiting for us. I'm gonna run out first. Maybe I'll draw their fire so you can run out."

Janet started to protest, but he cut her off. "I'm gonna run to my left. You come right behind me, but you run to your right, toward town. Get in the weeds next to the creek."

"Ray, you can't . . ."

He handed her the pistol. "Take this. Don't be afraid to shoot a man. They'll be trying to shoot you."

Hands trembling again, she took it, gripped it tightly.

"I'm not a praying man, Janet, but God bless you."

"Ray . . ."

"Good-bye."

Raymond Whitfield jumped over the pile of dirt and ran outside. He ducked sharply to his left, trying to get out of the firelight.

Guns boomed.

James Waggoner saw the fire. He heard the gunshots. Reining up, he realized the fire was in front of his family's old dugout, and the shots were coming from there. Someone was trying to kill someone, no doubt about that. Or had already killed someone. He turned the horse back to the creek and dismounted. He had to find out, and it would be better to go on foot, out of sight in the dark. Dropping the reins, he fumbled through the saddlebags until he found his powder flask and a box of lead balls and percussion caps. He stuffed all that in his hip pocket, and began making his way forward, cautiously, eyes straining in the dark.

The shooting stopped for a few seconds, then started again. Furious shooting.

Janet's mind and body snapped into action. Run to the right, Ray had said. Quickly, she scrambled over the pile of dirt, ran through the door, and ducked to the right, headed for the creek and the tall weeds. Her long dress was a handicap. She had to hold it above her ankles as she

211

ran. It snagged on the weeds and pulled at her, nearly pulling her down. Gripping the pistol, she stayed on her feet and ran.

For a moment, she thought she had escaped. Then a shout: "She's over there near the creek. She's gettin' away."

Guns roared. Lead bullets sang around her, clipped the weeds, and thudded into the ground. Half-crying and half-praying, she kept going. A bullet plucked at the dress near her knees. She stumbled over something in the dark and fell heavily onto her face.

She was as good as dead. She knew it. Three men were running at her. Looking back, she could see them clearly in the firelight. They would find her. They would shoot her to death. She couldn't just lie there. She had to try.

Lungs pumping, breath whistling, Janet started to get up, expecting a bullet in the back.

Another gun opened up.

Two loud reports came from somewhere west of her. A man's voice yelled, "Janet, stay down. Stay down, Janet." The gun boomed again.

She recognized the voice, but couldn't see him in the dark. Then, looking over her shoulder again, she saw one of the men in the firelight drop his pistol, spin around, and fall. Another cursed. "There's somebody over there. Somebody's shootin' over there." The two men still on their feet ran out of the firelight and disappeared in the dark.

Jim hurried up and dropped to the ground beside her. "Are you hit, Janet?"

"No." Her breathing was ragged, but she was calm. "I don't think so."

"Stay down. When you get up, that dress makes you easy to see."

Trying to get her breathing under control, she said, "Seems you're always coming along in the nick of time, James."

"I've been looking for you. You sure you're not hit?"

"I'm sure. But I think they shot Ray Whitfield. He's

212

probably dead."

"Uh-oh," Jim said, squinting into the dark, "they're not giving up." He aimed the Army Colt and squeezed the trigger. The heavy gun bucked and boomed. Fire shot out of the barrel. He cocked the hammer back and aimed again. The hammer fell, but the percussion cap failed to fire.

"Oh boy. Got to reload." Jim rolled over on his side and reached for the powder flask. "Lie flat, Janet. Don't move a muscle."

Fingers working as fast as he could move them, Jim tipped up the powder flask, pouring a measured amount into the neck of the flask. Then he poured it into the cylinder of the gun. He tamped a lead ball in place and put a percussion cap on one of the cylinder nipples. One chamber was loaded. He had to do that six times to completely reload the gun. He worked by feel, working desperately.

Janet saw one of the men coming toward them. He apparently hadn't located them yet in the dark, but he soon would. Jim was busy reloading his gun. In a few seconds the man would see them and shoot them. With Jim's gun unloaded they were helpless. Unless . . .

She realized she still had Ray Whitfield's pistol, and she raised up onto her elbows and pointed it at the advancing man. Gripping the gun with both hands, squeezing her eyes closed, she pulled the trigger.

Chapter Thirty-six

The explosion from Ray Whitfield's gun nearly deafened Janet and the gun nearly jumped out of her hands. But when she opened her eyes, the man was no longer there. Using both thumbs, she cocked the hammer, ready to fire again.

"Good shot," Jim whispered. "I'm almost ready." Finally, he snapped the cylinder into place and said, "There's more of them. They know where we are. We'd better move."

"Where? Where can we go?"

"Crawl backwards. Stay flat. Keep watching."

They crawled, inching backward, holding pistols in their hands. Janet's dress kept sliding up her legs and she had to repeatedly pull it down. They crawled, slithering like snakes. Backward.

It seemed like they had crawled a mile, but it was closer to fifty feet. Jim stopped. She stopped. He whispered, "I don't see or hear them. I wonder if they've given up."

"Do you think we can stand now?"

"Maybe. That light-colored dress of yours is easy to see. Tell you what — I'll stand, and you get behind me. Stay behind me." He stood, squinting into the dark. "All right, start walking. Go slow and don't make any more noise than you have to."

She stood too, and walked, slowly, carefully. Weeds pulled at her dress. Glancing back now and then to be sure Jim was following, she walked. He whispered, "Stop a minute. Listen." She stopped and turned toward his voice.

"I don't hear anything. I don't think they're following us. We can't be sure, though. Go ahead, but be careful."

They went on, pushing through the weeds, sometimes stumbling over downed tree limbs and uneven ground. "Wait," Jim whispered again. She stopped.

"I just thought of something. They're not following us on foot, but they might be waiting for us somewhere ahead. Yeah, they could have got on the road and got ahead of us. They know we're trying to get back to town. They might be just waiting for us ahead somewhere."

"What should we do?" Janet whispered.

"Well, I think we'd better stop here. Sit down. We'll stay here till daylight. Sit down, find a comfortable spot, and wait."

She sat in the weeds on her feet. Jim sat beside her. "Listen," he whispered. They listened. The only sound was the prairie breeze, rustling the leaves of a cottonwood. After a long moment, he whispered, "Do you know where we are?"

"Not exactly."

"We're close to the tree where . . . you know."

"Oh. I've got some news about that."

"What?"

"It's a long story. I think you know most of it."

"Yeah. Better wait to tell me. Better keep quiet awhile."

"Yes."

It was a long night. Twice, Janet had to shift positions. After two hours she found herself about to doze off. Jim had to shift positions too. "James?" she whispered.

"Yeah?"

"I'm still holding this gun, Ray Whitfield's gun, and I think it's cocked. How do I uncock it? I'm afraid I might accidentally pull the trigger."

"Let me have it."

She could barely see him in the dark, but she found his

hand and felt it take the gun from her. His hand felt warm and friendly in the dark. She wanted to hang onto it. But he pulled it away.

"James?"

"Huh?"

"How much longer until daylight?"

"Can't be much longer."

"Will we be safe then?"

"I think so. At least, if they're still around, we can see them. We can defend ourselves."

"We're only about half a mile from town. Do you think they'd try to shoot us this close to town?"

"Probably not, but I'm not sure. We might have waited here in the dark for nothing."

"No, I think you were right about staying here. In fact, I'll bet they're over there by the bridge, just waiting for us to come along."

"That's what I was thinking."

"James, I'm afraid Ray Whitfield is dead."

"He is? How did you happen to be in the dugout with him?"

"He . . . died trying to save my life."

"Why did he do that?"

She started to tell him, but decided that this was not the time or place. "It's . . . look, is the sky getting lighter?"

"Yeah. Over east. I believe it is."

They were silent while the eastern horizon gradually turned pale. A faint glow slowly appeared. The night breeze turned cool, and Janet shivered and hugged herself. She wanted to snuggle up to Jim, but she wasn't sure he would like that. The pale light grew brighter. She realized she could see the tree, then Jim's face.

Thin whisps of gray clouds hanging over the eastern horizon were turned purple by the light.

"It's beautiful, James. I never want to spend another night like this, but the prairie dawn is beautiful. It makes me realize the city is not the place for me."

"How about your schooling?"

216

"I want more education, but I want to come back here to teach."

"Yeah, it's sure pretty, all right. I never liked the city much either."

Shivering, she reached for his arm and hugged it to her breast. He didn't try to pull away. But he whispered, "As soon as we hear some life in town, we'll go."

"Yes," she whispered. "We should be safe now." She wanted to rest her head against his shoulder. She wanted his arm around her.

The top edge of the sun showed itself. Daylight was here.

"Do you think we can go now?"

"Yeah." He pulled his arm away from her and stood. He took her hand and pulled her to her feet. The stitches in his side stung, and he realized he was going to have to take them out soon. His gun was in its holster, and Whitfield's gun was stuck inside his gunbelt. For a brief moment, she leaned against him. His arms went around her. The top of her head came only to his shoulder. Then, embarrassed, he dropped his arms. "We can go now."

She decided she was going to hang onto his left arm whether he liked it or not, and she did. Suddenly he stopped. "Wait. Somebody's coming. Get down."

They dropped to the ground again and waited among the weeds. They heard men's voices. A man said, "We oughta get some hosses. No tellin' where all that racket came from."

"Why don't you go roust old Butler out and get some horses? I'm gonna walk a little farther."

Janet stood, smiling. "It's Sheriff Rogers."

The lawman saw her immediately, and directed his steps their way, pushing through the hogweeds and sunflowers. Jim stood and waited silently.

"Miss Carbaugh. What's going on? What was all the shooting about?" Eyeing Jim, he said, "Might have known you were mixed up in it."

Jim didn't know what to say, where to start explaining.

Janet opened her mouth to speak, but the sheriff cut her off. "I want to know all about it and I want to know right now."

Janet answered, "Some men tried to kill us. I'm afraid they killed Ray Whitfield."

"Why?" Sheriff Rogers's voice was demanding.

"All right." Janet reached into a pocket of her dress and pulled out two sheets of paper. "This will explain it. This will explain a lot of things. But I want James to read it first."

Jim took it from her and read. When he finished, he looked at Janet and at the sheriff, and read it again. Janet waited patiently. The lawman growled, "Well, what is it?"

Puzzled, Jim asked Janet, "When did he write this?"

"Back there in the dugout. Four men tried to burn us out and kill us. But I think he planned to go to Sheriff Rogers and tell him all about it and write out a statement there. He had paper and a pencil with him."

Rogers barked, "Tell me what?"

Jim handed the paper to Janet, who handed it to the sheriff. He read. While he was reading, Jim said, "I thought it was all Chester Tuttle's scheme. What made Whitfield confess like that?"

"When he learned that they tried to burn me to death, he decided the time had come to end the whole rotten affair."

"Well, I'll be . . ." Rogers had finished reading. He studied Janet's face, then he too read it a second time. "Well I'll be . . ." He didn't know what to say without swearing.

Janet said, "It answers some questions, doesn't it, sheriff?"

"It sure as hell — heck — does."

"You're in charge now," she said, "what's next?"

"Well, I . . . You say Ray Whitfield's dead?"

"I'm afraid he is. And there may be one or two others shot. Near the old Waggoner dugout."

"This is his gun," Jim said, handing over the pistol that

218

Janet had given him.

"Well." The lawman looked back toward town and saw two horsemen coming, leading another horse. Here comes some help. I'll send them over there to see what they can see." When the horsemen came up, the sheriff asked them to ride along the creek to the dugout, see what was to be seen, and report back. Jim said he was going to go get his horse. Rogers told the men to bring back any loose horses, and he told Jim to wait.

The lawman was silent, head down, thinking. Finally, he asked Janet, "Are you sure Ray Whitfield wrote this confession?"

"I'm sure. I saw him write it. Not only that, he told me all about it."

"His handwriting can be checked, you know."

"I hope you do get an expert to check it."

"I will — the prosecutor will. Meantime, I . . ." Rogers swallowed hard. "I guess I'm gonna have to arrest Chester Tuttle."

"He's at home," Jim said.

"I know. I never arrested anybody as important as he is."

"We'll go with you," Janet volunteered.

"No, I . . . Well, maybe it would help if you told him what Ray Whitfield told you. That and this paper ought to convince him to give himself up."

"Can we wait? I want to know about Ray. There's a small chance that he's still alive."

"All right, we'll wait."

Chapter Thirty-seven

They didn't have to wait long. The two riders came back, leading Jim's roan horse and four others tied head to tail. One of them, a tall, skinny man with a bobbing Adam's apple, reported, "Raymond Whitfield's dead. At least four bullets in 'im. Another'n is dead. He's the gent they called Case. Shot through the chest. And another's got a bullet in the leg. There was a fire in front of that cave, but it's burned itself out. No sign of anybody else."

"Get a wagon and bring them all in, will you?" Rogers said. "I've got another chore to do." To Janet, he said, "Come along."

"James is coming too."

"Not him. Oh, well." With a threatening look at Jim, he added, "But keep that shooting iron in its holster, understand."

It was a short walk to the Tuttle house. They led their horses and tied them at a hitchrail in front of the house. With slow, wooden steps, as if he dreaded doing what he had to do, Sheriff Rogers led the way onto the porch. The door opened before he could knock. Chester Tuttle came outside. He was dressed in a gray suit with cravat and a black Prince Albert coat. His eyes went from one of his callers to another and finally settled on the sheriff. Mrs. Tuttle came out too and stood behind her husband.

"What is this, Tom?"

"Uh, Mr. Tuttle, I'm afraid I'm gonna have to place you

220

under arrest."

The politician's face didn't change expressions. He spoke calmly, "Do you know what you're doing, Tom?"

"Yes, sir, Mr. Tuttle, I do."

"Why? On what charges?"

"I don't know what the attorney will call it. Maybe murder. I have to take you into custody. Here, read this." He handed Whitfield's written confession to the politician.

Tuttle read it hastily, then asked, "Where is Ray?"

"Dead."

"Oh. Then all you have here is this note, which could have been written by anyone."

"There's more. He told Miss Carbaugh all about it."

"I see. Hmm." Chester Tuttle handed the paper back to the sheriff. "Hmm." He bowed his head, seemingly thinking.

"I'm sorry to have to do this, Mr. Tuttle."

In a flash of movement, a small silver-plated pistol appeared in the politician's hand. His voice was steady, "Don't move. Don't any of you move."

Startled, Sheriff Rogers spoke in an unsteady voice, "What do you . . . what do you think you're doing, Mr. Tuttle?"

"Give me your guns. No, on second thought, you keep yours, Sheriff." To Jim he said, "Give me your gun."

Jim didn't move. The bore of the little revolver was pointed at his face. Tuttle was still calm. "Give it to me or I'll shoot another hole in your head. You can see it coming." His finger tightened on the trigger.

"Give it to him, James," Janet said. "He can't shoot all of us."

Jim handed it over, butt forward, careful to keep his finger off the trigger. Tuttle took Jim's big Colt, cocked it, and put the small revolver back inside his coat. "Now," he said, still calm, "everyone knows the Waggoner boy came here looking for revenge. He's about to shoot you both and try to shoot me. Only I am armed too, and I will shoot

221

him first."

"Now, just a minute," Rogers said. "You can't —"

The big bore of Jim's Colt was aimed his way. "You first, Tom."

The sheriff saw death coming. He squawked, "You can't —"

Then Mrs. Tuttle moved. Standing behind her husband, she suddenly grabbed her husband's gun arm, forcing it down. Jim moved, grabbing Tuttle's right wrist, holding it down. The Colt boomed, but the slug tore through the wooden floor of the porch. Sheriff Rogers moved, twisting the gun out of the politician's hand, then reaching inside his coat for the small gun.

Everyone stood back. Janet sighed with relief. Tuttle was beaten and he knew it. With a pained expression, he turned to his wife. "Why did you do that?"

The woman was near tears. "Why? Because I know what kind of man you are. I know you are capable of causing the deaths of innocent people. Do you think I don't know about your other wife in Denver? Do you think I don't know about the lie you have been living? I've been trying to pretend . . ." Her voice broke and she turned her back, sobbing.

Janet went to her, put her arms around her, and spoke softly.

They were on horseback, riding east along Apache Creek. Jim had protested, saying his horse had had a saddle on its back too long already. Janet had been persuasive, promising that she had a reason, and both horses would soon get some rest and good feed. All she would say at first was that they were going to the Bar W ranch house. Not until they had ridden past The Tree did she say more.

"Let me begin by asking you something, James. What are your plans? Where are you going from here?"

He stared at her a moment, puzzled, trying to figure out what was on her mind. "I don't know. Now that everybody knows — or soon will know — that my dad and uncle were innocent, I want to put up a monument, a big hunk of granite from the mountains. And I want some kind of message on it."

"Why, that's a grand idea. In fact, I'd like to help. We can go to Denver and have it chiseled to any size and shape you want. And while we're there, you can have a doctor attend to your wound."

"Yeah." He knew she had more on her mind, and he waited for her to say it. The horses walked slowly side by side on the wagon road, their heads down.

"And after that, James?"

"I don't know. My family was cheated out of two sections of land and over a hundred head of cattle, but that was eleven years ago. The land is all deeded now, and the cattle have died or been butchered. There's nothing for me here. I can't legally claim anything." He looked down at his horse's ears.

"I can."

"What?" His head swiveled toward her.

"Apparently no one told you. I am the adopted daughter of Raymond Whitfield." Before he could speak again, she went on, "My mother was a widow, and she married Ray when I was fourteen. I was raised on the Bar W."

While he was absorbing that, she told him all about it, ending with, "I am the only heir of Raymond Whitfield. I now own the Bar W ranch."

He was too surprised to speak.

"And as owner, knowing that two sections of the ranch and over a hundred cattle are rightfully yours, I can't let you just ride away. I couldn't live with myself if I did that. So, I'll deed two sections over to you, and you can cut out the cattle. Will that be fair?"

Flabbergasted, he stammered, "Why, uh, yeah, I guess, if that's what you want to do."

"That's what I want to do. But there's more. I want to go to school in Denver another year, and I need someone to manage the ranch. Will you do it? There's a spare bed-

223

room in the house, and you can live there."

"Why, uh . . ."

She was looking at her own horse's ears now. In a soft voice, she said, "After a year we can decide what permanent arrangements we want to make."

He had to swallow. "All right. Sure."

Her dress was torn and dirty and her dark hair was matted as she rode side by side with Jim Waggoner. Her brown eyes were wide, almost pleading. "We have a lot of details to work out, and I have to tell the ranch crew all about everything, but, James, I really need you."

Jim Waggoner rode silently until he had it all clear in his mind. Then he smiled. "Sounds like a good plan to me. I like it." His smile widened.

"I like it a lot."